<u>Castaway Bay</u>

The Fatherless Series - Book 2

By Kathleen Morris

Amazon Kindle Edition

Copyright 2025 by Kathleen Morris

Rouge Publishing

ISBN: 978-1-927828-66-3

Dedication

This book is dedicated to all those who have suffered through trauma. The Lord will restore everything the devil took from you.

1 Peter 5:10
"And after you have suffered a little while, the God of all grace, who has called you to his eternal glory in Christ, will himself restore,

KATHLEEN MORRIS

confirm, strengthen, and establish you."

Trust Him...and He will carry you through!

Table of Contents

THE STUNT

NOT IN A MILLION YEARS

THE FIGHT

SLEEP

FOOL OR NOT

NO SAFE PLACE

JUST SURVIVE

ALIVE

THE GETAWAY

I TOLD YOU

SORRY

THE HOARDER

GOB HOLE

CHOCOLATE BARS

THE HANDSHAKE

I TOLD YOU SO

PIGGYBACK

Jump

The 50-foot wooden fishing trawler rocked back and forth against the turbulent ocean as it neared Angoon, Alaska, in the dark of night. That pig was steering the boat. He could barely keep it afloat. *Figures!* He knew nothing about being a skipper.

Lily doubted he was even the rightful owner. He probably stole the boat, just like he stole everything else, including her. The two brothers kidnapped her from Anchorage, Alaska, over a year ago, fooling her into thinking they wanted to help her get off the streets.

They pretended they were street preachers, but they were anything but that. It didn't take her long to realize she was their latest victim.

Painful memories flooded in.

As the boat rose and fell in the water, Lily's stomach churned. Both the thought of what happened to her, and the ridiculous rollercoaster ride she found herself on, made her nauseous. Still, the deadly seas were not the only threat to her life; they were taking her to Angoon to be sold.

She wondered what the going rate for a fourteen-year-old blonde-haired runaway was these days. If it wasn't for her chubby, short stature, she was told they would have gotten double the price for her.

"You may have a pretty face," they told her, "but you're an ugly, fat, dwarf!"

Lily didn't care what they thought; she just kept scarfing down food any chance she got. The uglier and fatter the better, in her opinion. Maybe then they'd leave her alone. Nobody would want a blimp.

Her so-called stepfather made that fact clear just before her thirteenth birthday. He threw her out shortly after moving in with her mother, claiming she was costing him too much money on groceries. He got a kick out of calling her fatso, among other derogatory names, slapping her around, and treating her worse than the dog every chance he got.

She found all her belongings on the back porch one day when she came home from school. "Don't come back, you retard!" He shouted through the window. Her mother said nothing to defend her, like always. It was then she realized she was completely alone in this good-for-nothing world. The only one she could count on was herself.

Lily lived on a friend's couch after that, until social services got involved. They put her in a special needs group home just because she was a little slow. They claimed she had Williams Syndrome, whatever that was. What a joke! There was nothing wrong with her. Just because she resembled an elf didn't mean she was handicapped. Maybe she had superpowers. Wouldn't they be surprised if all she had to do was wiggle her nose and they would be dead?

Wishful thinking! That would have come in handy in the group home! The place was like a prison most days, and much worse than anything her stepfather ever dished out. Running away wasn't even a choice at that point. It was the only option she had to survive.

Options. Lily realized that was a foreign word to her. Why did all the other kids have opportunities, except for her? Why was she the only one who had to endure a miserable, pathetic childhood? Lily knew she wasn't the only one, but it sure felt like that.

She met plenty of homeless people, and it was a rough life. Living on the streets was dangerous, especially as a young girl. She slept on dirty cardboard and ratty old tarps the first few nights. Then, an elderly homeless woman took her under her wing for a few months until she met up with *the brothers.*

They were known on the street as the Preacher Boys.

"WAKE UP!" The younger brother kicked her leg. "You need to go down below, stupid! Don't you know the storm is too rough to stay out here? We want you safe."

Sure, you do.

Lily knew the only reason they wanted her to go below was to keep their precious cargo safe. She was their money train.

"Fine! I'm going!"

The yellow rain jacket she was wearing kept her warm as she huddled in the corner, watching the storm from the bow of the ship. She would have loved to stay out there longer. Lily felt strangely at peace in the storm for some reason. The mist that washed her face soothed her. It was as if the water was washing her clean.

And it was warmer than normal.

Anchorage was experiencing a mid-August heatwave when they left. She was thankful for that. It made the ocean inviting. At their last stop, she waded into the water until they shoved her back into the boat.

If only they had let her stay in the water a little longer, it would have soothed her aching back. She twisted it a couple of days ago, and it was still painful and throbbing.

"I told you to get below!" A voice shouted in the stormy dark. It was the younger brother again. His name was Derek. He had a mouth on him, swearing a list of profanities at her to get moving.

"I am!" she told him.

This time, she figured she'd better listen, *kind of.* What did she care? She moved to the stern of the ship and pretended to go below. As soon as he wasn't looking, she snuck into the corner and stayed above deck to continue watching the storm. Thankfully, he and his brother were too focused on steering to follow her around. She snuggled into an unlit corner and let the mist rain down on her face again.

Maybe it would cleanse her soul. That's what she needed. She'd give anything to start over. If only she could. If only she could get away from them.

Suddenly, Lily caught a light at the corner of her eye. She pushed back the hood of her rain jacket and squinted into the mist. It was a flicker. It was a lighthouse. Yes! *There!* Did they even realize how close to shore they were? Of course not. *Idiots!* They weren't sailors.

She could see an outcrop of rocks as lightning revealed the bay in front of them. It was only a few miles away. Practically close enough to touch.

Freedom!

Was it really that close? Maybe she could swim. Quickly, she looked around for a life jacket. She could simply float away. They would never know. By the time they went looking for her, she'd be long gone.

Or, dead.

Lily gulped hard. She decided to make her move. The rain pelted her rain jacket as she peered around the corner to make sure the coast was clear. They were still both at the helm, arguing this time, trying to keep the doomed trawler afloat.

They could drown for all she cared.

She quickly grabbed a life jacket and tied it to her round body. It was now or never. Against the rocking boat, she climbed over the side. She stood on the platform at the stern of the ship and sat down, immersing her legs in the raging water.

It was warm and inviting. It seemed like the ocean was calling her name as it slapped against her body. She could barely hang on as the trawler bounced and danced to the rhythm of the waves.

Jump, she told herself.

Then, as if it were the last thing she'd ever do, she slipped into the stormy ocean and disappeared into the night.

The Test

Kelly couldn't believe how beautiful Angoon was. It was everything she imagined and then some. It was their own little slice of paradise. The place she and Boone called home shortly after they got married five years ago today.

Life was blissful the first two years of marriage. Boone established a new business that had nothing to do with bears this time. After crashing his seaplane and then both of them nearly dying, he decided God wanted him to focus on something else: A fishing charter.

He got all the certifications and bought a fishing trawler with the insurance money from his bear guiding business. It was more than enough to start over.

Kelly sold everything she had in Toronto and pooled it together with her new husband and new life in Alaska. Together, they ran "Second Chance Charters."

It was very profitable.

Every week, tourists would fly in for a chance to catch the big one. Mostly, they enjoyed Boone's crazy stories and learning how to catch salmon. On occasion, they got to see whales and learn about Tlingit culture.

Kelly especially liked that part. She was fascinated with their culture and loved living amongst the Tlingit people in Angoon. She was proud of Boone's heritage, with his mother being part Tlingit. She sure wished she'd been able to meet her before she died.

Instead, Kelly spent most of her time with Boone's Aunt Sally. She was a lovely older woman who told her everything she needed to know about the mother-in-law she never got to meet. She had hoped to one day name their first child Rose, after Boone's mother, but so far, that was proving to be very difficult. She'd had four miscarriages in the span of three years, and it broke her heart every time. It also put a strain on their marriage and their faith, but they had pushed forward somehow, even after deciding they were done trying.

The fertility clinic they went to in Anchorage after their last miscarriage told her she would never have children because of her celiac disease. They told her she suffered from malabsorption as a child before being diagnosed, and that damaged her reproductive system. But getting pregnant wasn't the problem. Keeping it was.

Obviously, they were wrong because she was pregnant again. It shocked her to see a positive pregnancy test this morning, even while on birth control. She figured this miracle pregnancy must be about five or six months along already. How embarrassing. If the timing is correct, it's longer than all her other pregnancies.

She had her suspicions as each month rolled by, but every time she tested, it was always negative. Her cycles were so unpredictable since her last miscarriage seven months ago that she didn't give it another thought. She figured her body was just recovering from the repeated trauma, and it would take a while to get back to normal.

She remembered being put on antibiotics after her wisdom teeth removal in early spring. She was told the brand she was taking wouldn't interfere with birth control.

Well, they were wrong.

There was no question now. *Positive means positive.* She'd been experiencing morning sickness for quite some time, writing it off as a gluten issue again. She was hiding it from Boone for the most part, hoping it was just the flu.

It was definitely not the flu!

Besides, if she really were that far along, she'd never live it down. Nobody would believe she tested negative all this time. And what would cause that? A miscarriage, maybe? Something she didn't want to think about.

Maybe in her mind, she really knew she was pregnant and didn't want to accept it. Or, maybe it was a mental health issue. Maybe she knew, but she didn't want to miscarry, so she pretended she wasn't pregnant. The weight gain should have given it away, especially around her middle. Well, whatever the reason, she had an answer now.

Positive!

This time, Kelly decided she was going to be very careful with gluten cross-contamination starting today. She would not go out to any restaurants or eat any food not prepared by herself. Better safe than sorry. In her opinion, gluten poisoning was the cause of her other miscarriages. She could even pinpoint the time of the gluten exposure with the dates of each of her miscarriages.

Cross-contamination was the hardest part of being a celiac. Going to a restaurant wasn't worth it if she risked potentially being exposed, and she swore to never trust one again, no matter how much they convinced her it was safe.

They would have to find another way to celebrate special occasions instead of going out for supper. Kelly's mind remembered the pain. Before each miscarriage, they had visited a restaurant for someone's birthday or anniversary. At first, it felt like God was punishing them, but after talking to her pastor and receiving Aunt Sally's comforting advice, she realized God would never harm the people He loves.

Always, Aunt Sally's words popped into her head whenever she thought negatively about her misfortune. "You are a child of the King! The devil can't touch you!"

Words to live by. Literally!

"Earth to Kelly," Aunt Sally interrupted her thoughts. "What are you thinking about? You haven't touched your stew."

"I know," she took a breath. "I shouldn't have come."

"What do you mean? Of course, you should have. We always do lunch on Thursdays."

Kelly didn't know how to tell her. She didn't even want

to broach the subject. All those times before just flooded in. Instead, she started to cry.

Great! Her hormones were getting the best of her again.

"Hey, hey, hey!" Aunt Sally reached across the table and cradled her hands. "What's going on with you, my girl?"

Kelly pulled her hands away and wiped her tears. She took a breath and reached into her purse. *"This!"*

She showed Aunt Sally the news she hadn't even told her husband about. Two pink lines. She placed the pregnancy test on the table in front of the woman, hoping she had something uplifting to say about it.

"You're pregnant! Oh, Kelly, that's wonderful news!"

"Is it? What if it happens again?"

Aunt Sally sighed. "I don't want to pretend I have all the answers for you, honey, so I'll get straight to the point. It could happen again, but maybe it won't. If you're going to live your life worried, you'll miss the blessings. You can either let it break you or make you. We've been through this before. Trust that the Lord knows what He's doing."

Kelly sobbed, "I know. I do. I'm just so scared."

"I'll get the prayer team right on it."

"No! Don't! I haven't told Boone yet. I don't even know what to say to him. He's been so crushed over this whole thing. It was just as hard on him as it was on me. That's why we decided to stop trying and get our foster parents' license. You know that was our plan B, but then he backed out, and I was devastated all over again.

"I remember. But at least you don't need plan B anymore. Isn't that a good thing?"

"It is, but I'm not so sure Boone will be happy about another pregnancy. He's given up on having a family of *any* kind. He doesn't even want a dog."

"Oh, honey! He'll come around."

"I hope so, because he's pretty stubborn, you know. He's going to think I deliberately didn't take my birth control. *I did!* I don't understand it, Aunt Sally. How could something like this even happen?"

"Oh, it happens. When God wants something, He just does it. It's not up to us. Just sit back, let Him do what He wants, and He'll see you through. I'll tell the prayer team to keep it quiet. Right now, that baby needs immediate prayer. Not later."

Kelly agreed. The woman was wise, and she knew she was right about everything.

"Now, let's look at the blessings, shall we?" Aunt Sally beamed. "I'm going to be a grand-aunt again. My grandbabies may be in heaven, but they're all mine. And we're going to have grandbaby number five. That, my dear, is a complete blessing! Whether God decides to let this little one stay here or take him or her up to heaven, it doesn't matter. A life is a life, and that child in your belly should be celebrated."

Aunt Sally had a way of making her feel better. Her warm, loving soul was so compassionate that it brought her to tears *again*.

"How do I tell Boone?"

"My girl, tell him like it's the first time. *Celebrate!*"

"But not by going out to a restaurant, that's for sure! I don't trust them anymore. The gluten cross-contamination poisoned my body, so I couldn't carry them to term. I know that sounds crazy, but..."

"Shhh, my girl!" Aunt Sally interrupted her immediately. She tried to soothe her, but her concern was noticeable. She grabbed both of Kelly's hands again and prayed with her. She prayed for the baby's safety. She prayed for the strength to get through this. She prayed for Boone to take the news well. It was very heartwarming.

She felt better already.

"Now, let's celebrate by shopping online for some sweet little outfits. We can do that at least. I'll get my tablet. You've turned me into a frequent shopper, you know."

That made Kelly laugh. The woman knew nothing about online shopping until last year when she showed her how to do it for the artisan boutique she ran. It was quite the ordeal. "Okay, but I hope you don't do too much online shopping or you're going to spoil this little one." She patted her big tummy, realizing now that her weight gain wasn't from overeating or depression like she had thought.

"Now, that's my girl. Enjoy the blessings! God wants us to enjoy our lives, no matter how long or short He graces us with life."

"Thank you, Sally!"

This means more to me than you know.

The Curve Ball

It was supper time already, and Boone wasn't back yet. He spent the whole day with the tourists who flew in last night. He would be exhausted and hungry when he got home.

But he knew it was their anniversary. He promised they'd spend the evening together. That's why she cooked his favourite meal: Perogies and sausage.

It was Mary's special recipe. She was his old landlord from Juneau. She was in a nursing home now, and every time they went to Juneau, they would visit her. The place felt like her old stomping grounds.

Kelly used to be a nurse's aide in a Toronto nursing home before she met Boone. She remembered those days fondly. She used to work twelve-hour shifts back-to-back, taking care of the elderly. It was a lot of work, but she loved it. She especially liked making them feel special. It was more than just a job; it was a calling.

Back three years ago, she thought her calling was motherhood. She exchanged adult diapers for newborn diapers, though she never got to use them. They were still tucked away in the back of the closet somewhere; That, and a tiny sweatshirt that said, *Macho,* on the front of it. She and Boone picked it up at a garage sale during the first pregnancy. She couldn't bear to part with it.

"Throw it out!" Boone told her after the fourth miscarriage. He was so hurt after the loss, he barely spoke to her for a while. She realized miscarriages were not just hard on the woman. Men suffered too, just in a different way. That fact was a hard lesson to learn.

That's why she hid the sweatshirt. That's why she hid the diapers. That's why she hid her morning sickness. She didn't even tell Boone her suspicions, or that she was taking a pregnancy test every few weeks since the start of summer, just to be sure.

It was time to come clean.

Kelly realized the truth of the matter was, Boone would withdraw into his work. She did the same thing, slaving over paperwork. She handled the business side of things at home, as well as helped Aunt Sally out at the artisan boutique part-time.

It was easy to shut herself off emotionally so she wouldn't get hurt again. But, just in case, protection mechanisms always seemed to backfire with her. She knew Boone had tried it too, and it didn't work for him either.

They both went through therapy together to cope with the pregnancy losses. Kelly wondered what kind of therapy they needed now that they were unexpectedly pregnant again. Like Aunt Sally said, when God wants something, He just does it. She wondered what he was up to with this little surprise. It was a curveball indeed.

"*God, I'm just going to trust you on this one,*" she prayed.

She knew that's all she could do. She continued to pray for the baby's safety, for Boone's acceptance of this, and for them both to believe they will have a family, one more time. *One more time!*

Kelly stood at the kitchen sink with her apron on, staring out the window. There was her handsome ginger. He was walking up the driveway. He had let his red beard grow out extremely long. He loved that thing, spending hours and hours grooming it. All the expensive beard balms lined the shelves of their bathroom sink.

It was funny, really. Boone took so much pride in his beard; it was almost therapeutic. He hadn't cut it, except for small trims, since their first pregnancy loss. In a way, it was his way of coping, and she respected that. Boone seemed to hold on to things longer than she did. It took him a while to get to the other side.

Not that she had gotten to the other side already, but with this unexpected news today, it gave her a different perspective. Hope had started to grow since this morning.

"Can I keep this one, Jesus?"

The screen door screeched open as Boone stepped in. Kelly gulped hard and greeted her husband, "Happy Anniversary, babe!"

Boone leaned in to kiss her. "Happy Anniversary, Kells-Bells." A nickname that had grown on her over the years. A term of endearment.

"I'm sorry I'm late," Boone apologized. "Mr. Romano caught a big one. It was amazing! They're really pleased so far. They want to book with us for the next five years. Can you believe it? Guaranteed income. Not only that, but he said he has about ten clients who are looking for an experience just like this one. Ten Kelly! Did you hear me?"

"I heard you."

"Well, your excitement is underwhelming. What's wrong?"

Kelly decided rather than dragging this out, she would get it over with right away so they could focus on celebrating their anniversary. Hopefully, it would end well, or she would be eating all these perogies herself. Not like it hadn't crossed her mind. She was starving. If she didn't eat something soon, she'd be running to the toilet.

"Sit," she said.

Boone was apprehensive. "Is this good or bad?" He sat beside her on the old navy couch they'd had since they first got married. The very spot they sat when she told him she was pregnant four other times.

"Um... can we sit in the kitchen instead?"

"What's wrong with here?"

Kelly got up, took her husband by the hand, and led him to the prepared table. She wanted a different perspective. "This sofa's had its days. I want to sell it."

"Why? That's what you wanted to tell me?"

Kelly bit her lip. "No, I-I...have other news."

Boone settled into his kitchen chair, distracted by the meal. His mouth was watering at the sausages and perogies laid out in front of him. The candles she had decorated the table with were lit and flickering. The mood was romantic, yet her stomach didn't know it.

Nausea and dizziness hit her suddenly as bile rose in her throat. She could feel and taste it rising against her will. Kelly moaned as she cupped her mouth, eyes wide as she raced to the bathroom and puked in the toilet. She knelt on the floor and embraced the toilet bowl until she was finished with the unsightly mess.

"Honey! Again?" Boone followed her to the bathroom. "Maybe we'd better call Aunt Sally. I think we need her medical expertise. Either that, or we need to take a trip to Juneau to see the doctor. You've been like this on and off for a while now. I'm starting to get worried. Maybe you got the flu or something."

Kelly wiped her mouth with her sleeve. "It's not the flu!"

"Well, then what is it?"

She couldn't hide her emotions any longer. "I'm pregnant!" She bawled uncontrollably as she sat there on the bathroom floor.

"What?"

"I know!" She bawled again. "I took a pregnancy test this morning. It was positive. SEE!" She grabbed it off the bathroom counter and showed him.

"But you're on the pill. We've been more than careful. It would take a miracle to get pregnant with the precautions we take. Test again! It's gotta be wrong!"

At that point, Kelly knew Boone wasn't going to be able to handle this very well. He was already denying it. *Jesus, help!*

Then, Kelly remembered what Aunty Sally told her today. *Tell him like it's the first time: Celebrate the new life!* "Sit down beside me, my love!"

Boone dropped to the bathroom floor and sat against the

wall beside her. He combed his fingers through his long beard repeatedly. It looked like he was shocked. He stared into space and said nothing.

"Sweetheart," she sobbed, "Say something!"

Boone just kept shaking his head like he didn't believe it. The two of them sat in silence. Kelly reached for his hand and held it for the longest time. It wasn't a place where two people should stay for long, but Kelly didn't care. The moment wasn't wasted. It was necessary for healing.

And this was healing.

Finally, Kelly decided to speak. "I want you to know something. THIS...is a miracle. THIS...is a blessing. THIS...is a life! Let's celebrate it like it's the first time."

Kelly pulled Boone's hand to her belly and made him feel it. "Here! This is our baby!" The bulge was very evident. The baby was real. The blessing was theirs to enjoy if they wanted to.

Boone suddenly burst into tears.

Kelly squeezed his hand. "I know, my love, I know!"

The two of them cried together on the bathroom floor until they had no more tears left in them. They prayed together. They held each other. They prayed again and again, asking God if they could keep this one this time.

Finally, hope started to light up Boone's face. "Well," he sniffed, wiping his nose. "Enough of that! If we're going to do this, we're going *all-in.* We're having a baby, Miss Kells-Bells! Better get ready to get fat!"

"I already am!"

"I noticed!" Boone teased.

"You brat!"

They both held each other and kissed.

"Now, let's get off this dirty floor and get you cleaned up. We have some celebrating to do. Besides, I want those perogies!"

Kelly grinned, *Now that's my man!*

S.O.S

Lily crawled to shore in the early morning dawn as the sun peaked above the horizon. She lay there with excruciating back pain. The water slapped against her body with seaweed stuck to her yellow rain jacket. She knew she had to get out of there, but how?

Her back was on fire.

Seagulls laughed at her as she lay there moaning. Every few minutes, the pain would get stronger. She really did it this time. Not only was her back twisted, but every muscle in her body ached. She had to get off the beach.

By now, the brothers would be looking for her.

Though the warm August fog hid her for now, she knew it wouldn't be for long. It was only a matter of time before the sun would burn it off and reveal her whereabouts.

Come on, Lily, she told herself. *Move your big butt!*

With the storm long gone and the waters calm, all she could hear was the wind and the waves. It was calming as she forced herself to sit up. A lumpy orange starfish sat on the sand next to her, distracting her from the pain that crept up her back again.

"Oh, that hurts!"

It was cramping up more now than ever. She didn't know how she was supposed to climb up the hill to the lighthouse when she could barely move a muscle. All she knew was that she had to try. She rolled over on all fours and held that position as another strong pain attacked her body. A disk must be out.

"Come on! This pain is ridiculous!"

Lily waited for the cramping to stop, and then she made

her move. She stood shakily on her legs and used a big rock for support. Now all she had to do was make it up that hill. Surely there was someone up there who could help her.

Step by step, she moved past the reeds, the rocks, the weeds and the grass until she got to the top of the hill. It had only taken her a few minutes. Not as long as she thought. Her back only acted up a few times, but now she desperately needed the bathroom. It felt like a bowling ball was between her legs.

Constipation always made her feel like this.

She looked around for any signs of life, but the whole place seemed empty. Maybe they were sleeping. It was early morning after all. Lily yelled, "Hello?" She saw a house, but it was all boarded up. *Was there seriously nobody living here?*

"Hello?"

All she could see was a boarded-up house on a hill, and what looked like a mini lighthouse. The light was working, but it seemed automated. A large circle sat a few feet away from the house. Maybe it was a helicopter landing pad.

Lily figured it was an abandoned lighthouse. Maybe at one point someone lived there, but it was probably automated now, like everything else these days. Someone probably came to check on it once in a while. That could be why the helicopter pad was there.

If she was going to get help, she'd have to try and break into the house. Maybe there was a radio in there. Surely there had to be a way to reach someone.

Lily ripped off her lifejacket and dragged it with her. She got to the boarded-up house and realized she wasn't getting in the windows. She moved to the doors, and they were both locked with a padlock. *Great! Now what?*

An old, washed-out security logo was marked on the door, which meant the system was probably obsolete. At least she didn't have to worry about that, but maybe she could break the door down somehow.

Suddenly, the pains struck her back again. This time, her belly hurt as well. What was the matter with her? She tried to breathe, but the pain was too intense. She sat on the step and put her head between her legs. *Breathe!*

It was all she could do to catch her breath. She panted and moaned. Either she had to take a big dump or something was terribly wrong with her. Her back would need extensive work. Didn't people go to a back doctor for things like this? A chiropractor? She'd have to ask for one if she could only get into the house and call for help.

Then, on the ground, Lily noticed someone had dropped some long staples and nails all over the ground. Roofing supplies sat in a heap concealed by the overgrown flower bed. It looked like someone had done some renovations and didn't clean up the mess.

It didn't take a brain surgeon to realize this was her opportunity. The one thing she knew how to do was pick a lock. She learned how to do it when she was living on the streets. The old lady she was staying with taught her how. She used the technique to break into her home after her stepfather kicked her out. They didn't even know she had stolen money from the drawer, and grabbed a few things from the house that she needed.

Again, the pains came. This time stronger than the last. The sooner she could get inside, the better. Hopefully, there was a bathroom and a bed. She needed both desperately.

Finally, the throbbing stopped, and she was able to pick the lock open. She rambled up the stairs to the kitchen. Then she found a bathroom, thank goodness! That's what she needed the most right now. Hopefully, there was toilet paper because she knew this was not going to be good.

The pink and mint green bathroom looked like it was from the fifties. It would have to do. There was no running water, but at least there was an old, worn towel. The toilet paper roll was half used up, but at least it was something.

Lily ripped her yellow rain jacket off, threw it on the floor in a hurry, and pulled her wet jeans down to her stocking sand-caked feet. Before she sat down, she realized she was covered in blood. *What on earth?*

She didn't get a period. Her mother told her she had PCOS or something strange like that. She was always so vague about it when she asked her questions. Apparently, it was hereditary, and that meant she didn't have to go through female stuff. She never paid much attention to it after that. All she knew was that she didn't need pads or tampons. *Ever!*

But what was this now?

Something was seriously wrong with her. She was right. She'd have to look for a radio to call for help as soon as she was done in the bathroom. Maybe she'd punctured a kidney or ripped an intestine or something serious like that.

As she sat on the toilet, the pains hit her again. This time, pushing her constipated bowels felt like the only option she had. It gave her momentary relief until another wave of cramping hit her again.

Hopefully, soon, the agony would end. She moaned and groaned as she laboured to get the thing out. It was utter torture.

Then, suddenly, something plopped in the toilet. It was instant relief. Lily sighed and reached for the toilet paper when she heard a strange noise coming from the bowl. It sounded like an animal. A rat better not be in there!

She quickly lifted herself off the toilet, but something dangled from her. She ignored it to check the bowl for the rat first. Instead, what she saw was the bloodiest mess she'd ever seen. She nearly fainted at the sight of it. *Gross!*

Then, from within the bowl, she heard a squeak again. It was something caught in the mess. She didn't want to touch it. The thing could die in there for all she cared. What was it doing inside a toilet bowl in the first place? Maybe getting a drink. But there was barely any water in there in the first place.

And what was this rope hanging from her bottom, intestines?

She dropped to her knees and heard a distinct gurgle from within the bowl. Maybe it wasn't a rat. It was something else. She wiped some toilet paper across the contents and saw a bulging, round object. Then a squeak. Then an unbelievable wail.

IT WAS A BABY!

She screamed hysterically, gasping and choking. Her stomach churned as the room started spinning. The bathroom sink served to steady her so she didn't faint.

But it was too late.

Lily's body crashed to the floor.

A puddle of blood expanded beneath her.

Double Trouble

I t didn't even matter that Mr. Romano was expecting Boone to take him out fishing again; this was more important. He was taking the day off. He explained the situation and comped him an extra day. The fishing party was thrilled about the baby news.

Boone was hesitant at first about sharing that they were expecting, but now he was telling everyone he ran into. "We're having a baby!" No more fear. He and Kelly were going all-in this time. If God gave them another baby, it was a miracle. He was going to praise the Lord no matter what happened.

After taking several more home pregnancy tests last night and seeing two bold pink lines every time, Boone was confident it was correct. Not only that, his wife exposed her belly. Sure, he'd noticed she had put on a lot of weight since their last miscarriage, but never in a million years had he guessed she was pregnant.

They decided shortly after losing their fourth that it was too painful to try again. It was a hard decision, but they decided to wait a couple of years before deciding if they would ever try to have a baby again. Boone doubted they would, but Kelly wanted to leave the option open just in case they changed their minds. If it were up to him, he would have gone in for that vasectomy when he scheduled it six months ago. The last miscarriage had nearly destroyed their marriage and his faith.

But God is good.

The Lord got them through it, and counselling helped a great deal too. It was a slow recovery for both of them, but little by little they started to heal.

Just when he had given up on ever being a father, God had something else in mind. This was a complete surprise. It proved to him that God was in control, not him. Boone was fine with that. He was ashamed to think he ever could.

But to have Kelly so far along in her pregnancy worried him. Yet, he told himself he wasn't going down that path again. Worry was fear, and fear was not of God. He had to make a cognitive choice to avoid it at all costs.

Their counselling sessions gave him tools for his toolbox, but it was up to him to use them. It's something he and Kelly struggled with, but they were working on it. He realized it was a new kind of journey now.

Boone couldn't believe he hadn't noticed how big her belly was already. He was ashamed he hadn't touched his wife in over a month. They were still working through some issues, and she was always so tired. Now he knew why.

Lord, please help me to be a better husband, he prayed.

In his defence, he'd been running fishing expeditions back to back all summer long, and she had spent the last week of July and the first week of August in Toronto visiting an old friend she used to work with. They were both busy and hadn't had a lot of time together. He knew that was just an excuse, but he felt better telling himself that. The truth was, he had to work harder on his marriage. They both vowed to do that last night, when they celebrated their anniversary together.

It was hard to believe they'd been married for five years now. It felt like yesterday when she stood at the altar with him, barefoot in the sand. They had a beach wedding on the shores of Angoon, Alaska, on a lovely, hot August day like today. They flew to Juneau shortly after, and spent their honeymoon in a beautiful oceanfront cabin rental.

Who would have thought, five years later, they'd be in the same place getting an ultrasound. Their 3 p.m. appointment at the Bartlett Regional Hospital in Juneau was difficult to swing, but Dr Thomas said he'd squeeze them in for sure. He knew them well and took care of Kelly through each miscarriage.

He was a blessing.

She didn't even mind the flight in. She was a nervous flyer after the seaplane crash six years ago. It seemed a distant memory now. He was just thankful they made it through that horrific trauma, unscathed. It could have ended much worse, but instead, he got a second chance with her.

What was a bum like him doing with an angel like her, anyway? To this day, he hasn't felt worthy. She was more than he deserved. Yet, God gave her to him. She was his beautiful wife now, and she looked so pretty waiting for the doctor on the examination table.

"Earth to Boone," she chuckled. "You okay?"

"I'm more than okay." He kissed her softly. "We're having a baby!"

"Well, I hope it's not actually today. I have a few more months to go, you know."

They both chuckled as Dr Thomas came in the door. He stopped in his tracks and smiled. "Well, well, well, my favourite couple. Looks like we're in for a treat today. You two ready for this?"

Kelly said, "No."

Boone said, "Yes."

They looked at each other and laughed.

"Well, sounds about right," Dr Thomas winked.

He rolled a portable ultrasound machine to Kelly's bedside and stopped to talk to them before he got started. He was a kind old gentleman. They didn't make doctors like him anymore. He was old-school; the kind that would make a house call if you asked him.

"Now, you two," he said, "I want to cut to the chase. This isn't your first rodeo. Chances are, we see a baby today. However, there's a chance we don't."

Kelly gasped. Boone swallowed hard. He wondered why the doctor decided to lead with this. He expected him to be more positive.

"What do you mean? You mean she might not be

pregnant?" Boone asked.

"What I mean is, we've been through this a few times. Kelly, you've had miscarriages between the seventh and tenth week, four times in a row now. We didn't even get to your first ultrasound, at least not while you were still pregnant, anyway. The ultrasound we did after your last two miscarriages showed some scar tissue. It might be an issue now. I just want to warn you before we start."

"But, look at my belly, it's big. Are you saying it might just be scar tissue?"

"I'm saying you might not be as far along as you think. It's highly unlikely that you would continuously test negative and still be pregnant."

"But, it was positive yesterday," Boone said. He was starting to get annoyed now. What was the doctor saying, that her stomach was big because of scar tissue? That she wasn't really pregnant? Or, maybe she was only a few weeks, still in the window where miscarriage was likely. He couldn't go through this again.

Do not fear, for I am with you.

God's words echoed through his mind. He decided to choose to be calm. He squeezed Kelly's hand and prayed under his breath.

"I don't want to upset you guys. I just want you to be prepared for anything we see on the ultrasound. Good or bad. Both are likely. You know this. You've been through a lot. I hope I can bring you good news today, but you need to prepare yourself for the worst."

Kelly bit her lip. Boone just squeezed her hand harder. They both nodded at the doctor. "Let's do it."

The doctor placed a hand on Kelly and nodded. "Okay then, let's look at what we have." He booted up the ultrasound machine, lifted Kelly's shirt, and lowered her pants below her hip, exposing a protruding belly.

"My-my, you do have quite the bump, don't you? Hmm." The doctor furrowed his brow. He squeezed gel on Kelly's stomach and rolled the ultrasound wand around.

Boone knew Kelly had put on about ten pounds after each miscarriage, but he didn't realize how much that added up to until now. She was a lot bigger than the skinny girl he had met over six years ago. That was a good thing, though, because she looked anorexic before.

Suddenly, Boone heard a rhythmic gurgling sound.

"And that would be the heartbeat," the doctor smiled widely.

Boone yelped so loud they could hear him down the hallway. Kelly gasped, "That's the heartbeat? Boone! It's our baby!"

"Looks like you have a viable pregnancy after all. Let's just take a good look at your little one." He examined the ultrasound more closely. He told them he wanted to take measurements and thoroughly investigate. "If we're dealing with scar tissue as well, I want to know where it is and how much." The doctor wouldn't let them see the screen yet. He silently clicked away with his mouse for a long time, rolling the ultrasound wand through the gel on her stomach in complete silence.

Both Boone and Kelly waited with wide eyes and didn't say a word. Boone prayed under his breath that everything would look okay.

The doctor moved the wand around. He measured and looked confused. "Hmmm, you're definitely a lot further along than I thought."

"I told you," Kelly looked at the doctor, and then to Boone.

"Yes, you *did* tell me."

"So then, why was I getting negative pregnancy tests until yesterday?"

Then, the doctor suddenly looked surprised. He cleared his throat and smirked. "Aha, I think I just solved the mystery. Have you ever heard of the hook effect?"

They both shook their heads.

Boone was puzzled by the doctor's behaviour. He better not mean something's wrong. They heard the heartbeat already.

That meant they had a live baby in there. "What is a hook effect?" Boone asked point-blank.

"Well, when your HCG is too high, a pregnancy test can become overwhelmed and it reads incorrectly. It registers as a false negative in the first few months because it can't handle the high concentration of HCG until it comes down a bit. It's very rare. I haven't seen one case in my entire practice."

"Well, what makes high HCG?" Kelly asked.

The doctor cleared his throat again and turned the monitor toward them. "The reason you had high HCG levels until recently was...well...there's no easy way to put it. "High levels are associated with multiples."

"Multiples?" They both repeated the word in unison.

"What do you mean, multiples?" Boone asked, alarmed.

The doctor beamed. "YOU'RE HAVING TWINS!"

Boone and Kelly both screamed!

"Boy, for a minute there, doc, I thought you were going to say we were having a litter or something, like three or four." Boone joked a little too loudly.

The doctor laughed. "Well, you know, you might be surprised how they can hide behind their siblings sometimes." He continued to laugh.

Both Boone and Kelly's eyes went wide.

"You're joking, right?" Kelly looked shocked. "There are only two!"

The doctor roared this time. He leaned in to show them the ultrasound. "Look at your little blessings. Yes, there are only two. I'm sorry, I couldn't resist. See? Baby number one and baby number two. That's it. Double trouble, but not a litter." He winked at them both.

Boone was in shock even at the news of twins. He was thankful for God's blessing, but he didn't need a baseball team. He chuckled at the thought of it.

"Do you want to know what sex they are?"

Boone looked at Kelly. "What do you want to do, my love?"

"I never knew what the other four were." Tears welled in

her eyes. "It's something I've always wondered about. Can we find out now?"

Boone squeezed her hand and nodded. "Looks like that's a yes."

The doctor squinted at the screen through his bifocals and went on. "Well, first, I'll tell you they both look perfect. I don't even see any scar tissue. Remarkable. I see about twenty-four weeks of gestation. Incredible. You should feel them kicking already. You have, haven't you, my dear?"

"I feel so stupid. I thought it was gas."

"Sometimes, the mind plays tricks on us. We don't want to believe something, so we pretend it isn't happening. My dear, it's normal after so many miscarriages. You're afraid to hope. You know what I'm saying, don't you?"

Kelly nodded. She brushed away her tears and looked at Boone. He understood what the doctor was saying, too.

"Right now, I want you two to be excited. It's okay to hope again. This is a huge accomplishment for you guys to be so far along. Congratulations to you both. And it looks like they are identical, too. How lovely for you."

"Wow! Identical!" Boone smiled. "That's impressive!"

"Now, would you like to know what you're having?"

"YES!"

The doctor laughed again. His excitement was contagious. Boone was thankful to have such a loving doctor who actually cared. He was dragging this out deliberately, but they didn't mind one bit. It would go down in the history books as a blessed day.

"Okay, well, I've held you in suspense long enough. Let's just take one more listen to those beautiful heartbeats, shall we?"

THUMP SQUISH, THUMP SQUISH, THUMP SQUISH.

Boone was in awe. Kelly cried, and the doctor couldn't stop smiling.

"Mom and Dad, meet your baby girls!"

The Thing

By the time Lily came to, she was flying through the air in a helicopter. She felt dizzy and cold. Her teeth were chattering uncontrollably, even though a heated blanket kept her body warm as she lay on a stretcher. She had an oxygen mask on, and all she could do was listen to the EMTs as they talked amongst themselves.

"Lucky for her, the maintenance staff got the security notification right away. Quite the training mission, isn't it, you guys? We weren't even supposed to go up this morning."

"I think she's awake," a woman said.

"How's the baby?"

Was she dreaming? Did they just say baby? Lily went in and out of consciousness, wondering where they were taking her. She was still shivering.

Monitors beeped and alarms went off as they whirred through the air. Lily could hear someone on the radio, talking about landing. Where were they landing? She had no idea what was happening and where they were taking her.

It felt like she was in an elevator. Her stomach was nauseous and she was about to puke. But with the oxygen mask, it made it difficult. What if she puked in it? Lily moaned as an EMT rushed to her side and removed her mask. They turned her to the side as she puked into a bucket. Then they put her mask back on and pulled up the warm blanket.

They looked young, like they were students. Maybe they were learning, and she was the guinea pig. At least they were nice. One of them rubbed her arm and said, "You're okay, sweetheart. We're almost there."

Tears escaped the corners of Lily's eyes as she began to remember what happened. She didn't want to know about the baby. She didn't even want to see it.

The chopper landed on the helipad as the pilot announced they had arrived at Bartlett Regional Hospital in Juneau. Then, once the engine was shut down, they took that *thing* out of the chopper first. She could hear it cry, but she didn't care. As far as she was concerned, it should have died in the toilet.

Lily started to cry. She couldn't control her emotions. She was shaking uncontrollably, hoping they would take her out of the chopper soon. They just left her there, forgotten and abandoned like everyone else in her life had done.

Where were they? They were taking so long.

It felt like a million years while she lay on the stretcher waiting for them to come get her. All their attention was on that *thing*. She mattered too. What was wrong with them? She was so cold she couldn't stop shaking.

"Lily ripped off her mask and shouted, "Someone get me out of here!"

A young EMT came running back and shoved her oxygen mask back on against her will. She didn't want the thing on. It was hurting her face. "It's okay, we're almost ready for you, sweetheart," the woman said.

Stop calling me sweetheart.

Lily just wanted out. She shivered and cried, feeling completely helpless. All she could do was moan and make noises, so they took her seriously.

Finally, they wheeled her out and into a doorway, down a long hallway and into some bright lights. Too bright for Lily. They bothered her more than the mask. She moaned and cried, kicking her legs this time. Maybe someone would listen.

"Fourteen-year-old special needs female delivered in the field. In a toilet, actually. At the old lighthouse. Mild bleeding is stabilized. Unconscious when we arrived. Vitals are good now, but she's still in shock. Delivered a full-term baby boy. The Apgar score was good considering where we found him. Didn't even need oxygen. We kept him toasty warm. He's a little fighter."

Lily was brought into a busy hallway, and a doctor and some nurses took over from the EMT who told them all about her embarrassing situation. "Miss, do you know where you are?" they asked her.

She didn't want to talk to them, but she supposed that was the only way they could help her. After all, she needed them to keep her safe from the brothers. They would be looking for her by now.

"My name is Lily," she said.

"Well, Miss Lily, you have a healthy baby boy."

That was the last thing she wanted to hear. She wished she could tell them it wasn't hers, but they wouldn't believe her now. Not with the evidence. She wished she could have left it there. She didn't want the thing, anyway.

She didn't know whose kid it was; that was the truth. It could have been from any of the smelly old men she was forced to entertain. They were all the same. If she had known it was in there, she would have tried to get rid of it earlier.

Now it was too late.

One thing was for sure: Lily didn't want the thing. It was hard enough to keep herself safe. How could she keep a baby safe? Why would she even want to? Nobody protected her when she needed it the most, that was for sure.

"Why didn't you take her to post-partum?" an old nurse scolded them.

"We tried, but you're full."

"Well, not anymore. I just discharged someone. Now get her out of my hallway."

Lily thought the woman was mean. She was glad they were moving her out of the noisy area with bright lights. They rolled her into a quiet room at the end of the hall. Nobody was in it but her. *Good.* All she wanted to do was be alone anyway.

The large windows overlooked the parking lot, giving her something to keep her mind off what was happening. They were changing her bedding and cleaning her up. It was awful and very degrading. She didn't bother to say a word until they were done.

The nurses poked her hand and hooked her up to an IV, then hung a bag of something on a tall silver pole. She programmed a computer box on the pole, and it started making funny pumping sounds. Then, the nurse covered her with warm, clean blankets, and she felt all tucked in. It was a good feeling. The first good feeling she had felt in a long time.

"There, now you're all cleaned up. We'll be back to check on you in a bit. If you need anything, just press the button."

The nurse turned off the light and drew a long curtain around her. "Now, try to get some sleep; everything will feel much better when you wake up."

Lily doubted that.

Roommates

W e're going to admit you for a few days," Dr. Thomas told Kelly. "Now, I know you said you'd rather not, but I want to see these levels rise first. I wasn't expecting your vitamin D to be so low. We need to fix that for these babies you're carrying."

Kelly wasn't happy that she couldn't go home with Boone. They were just about to leave after their ultrasound when a nurse stopped them. That's when Dr Thomas advised her about her blood test being off.

"I'm always low in vitamin D. It's just part of my celiac disease. I usually take D3 every day, but I ran out last week."

"Kells, why didn't you tell me?"

Kelly fumed. They were making a fuss over nothing. She started to cry. "I'm not an invalid, you know. I just forgot to buy my vitamin pills, for Pete's Sake. It's not a big deal."

"Well, actually, it is now. You're pregnant," the doctor told her. "You haven't taken any prenatal vitamins. You're low in D and Iron, and your electrolytes are low as well. You need to take this seriously. I know you don't want to stay in the hospital, but it's an order. Besides, I would like to run some more tests."

"What tests?" Kelly asked.

"Well, since you haven't had any prenatal care for 20 weeks, we're behind. We're going to do a level two ultrasound to scan for abnormalities, and we need to do more bloodwork for you and the babies, and I want to do a genetic test. I'll have a glucose test done too while we're at it. Kelly, I know this sounds alarming, but considering your history, I want to be very thorough. You have a high-risk pregnancy."

"But, everything's okay though, right?" Boone asked, standing there ready to go home without her. She had the same question.

"Yes, yes!" The doctor told them, "I'm just making sure it stays that way."

Dr. Thomas smiled and reassured them that everything was okay, and then left the hospital room she had been put in. It was a big room with only two beds. Large windows looked out over the parking lot, and someone was sleeping in the first bed. Kelly couldn't tell who because the curtains were drawn. Probably a new mom. She was in the postpartum section of the maternity ward after all.

After the doctor left, Boone reassured her that everything was fine. He'd have to take a charter back to Angoon right away without her. There was nothing she could do about it. She wanted her babies to be healthy too; she just didn't anticipate a hospital stay. It brought back a lot of painful memories.

"I have to finish out the week with Mr. Romano. He and his crew are expecting to go out again tomorrow, and I have no choice. I also want to make sure he signs with us for the next five years, like he said he would. Hopefully, those clients of his sign as well. Babe, this is our livelihood."

"I know...I just wish I didn't have to be *here*."

"It's not like before. This is different, Kells."

"I know. We have two babies. Can you believe it, Boone? I'm shocked!"

"So, am I, but this is our second chance, babe. Well, more like fifth, but you know what I mean. Those heartbeats were epic!"

Kelly felt the same way. There was nothing like that. She clutched her baby bump and smiled. It was more than a blessing, it was a gift!"

They prayed quietly together before Boone left. She made sure he would update Aunty Sally right away. She was on pins and needles. A text wouldn't do it justice. Kelly wanted to tell her in person, but letting Boone do it was the next best thing.

After all, she was his aunt. But she and Sally had become fast friends. In fact, Kelly considered her to be her only friend. She had trouble in that area. That's why she deliberately went to visit an old work friend in Toronto a few weeks ago. No more burning bridges, the therapist said.

The trip was a distant memory. She had fun, but felt terrible. Now she knew why.

Kelly sighed as she waved goodbye to her husband, wondering how many days it would be before she saw him again. Hopefully, it wasn't going to be long.

After lying there for about an hour, a loud charge nurse came bursting into her room with another nurse. "Why isn't she in Antepartum like she's supposed to be! Who authorized her to be put in here?" The woman was so loud that she was going to wake up the woman sleeping next to her.

"Dr. Thomas himself. He authorized that Mrs. McKenzie be put in here. Antepartum is bursting at the seams, and he said she could stay a few days here."

"A few days? What on earth for!" The charge nurse was burly and loud. She didn't seem all that nice in Kelly's opinion. Hopefully, she wouldn't be her nurse.

"Is there a problem?" Kelly perked up.

The two women didn't answer her and stepped out of the room to talk. Then the nice one came back in and discussed the situation with her. "We're just on maximum capacity right now. I guess the other nurse thought you should be in the Antepartum unit. They monitor pregnancies. This ward is for moms who have already delivered."

"Oh."

"But don't you worry, we'll get this all straightened out. "Dr. Thomas didn't want you bumped to another floor, so he gave strict orders to keep you here before he left. He talked to me directly, so don't you worry."

"Will there be a baby in this room?"

"Well...I'm not sure. It depends on what happens with the other mom."

"I CAN HEAR YOU!" A voice on the other side spoke loudly out of turn.

The kind nurse pulled open the curtain encircling the other mom and introduced them. "This here would be Lily, and..."

Just then, an alarm went off down the hall. "Sorry, girls, I have to go!" She darted out of the room in a hurry. Probably someone's monitor went off. It reminded Kelly of the days she worked in a nursing home. It was more like a hospital with the same bells and monitors going on. She missed nursing, even if she was only an aide.

The late-day sun burst through the window, catching the other mom right in the eyes. It was at that time, Kelly fully realized this was just a child. She tried not to show her alarm, but she guessed it was written all over her face.

"You can say it. I'm too young to have a kid."

"No, I-I wasn't..."

"Nice try, lady. I can see it all over your face. Keep your judgments to yourself, why don't you. I didn't even know I had the stupid thing in me."

Kelly was shocked now. She didn't know what to say. For a moment, she would hold her tongue. She had to choose her words wisely. The poor elfin-faced kid couldn't be anything more than thirteen, though she sounded much younger. Her chipmunk voice made her seem more like an eight-year-old, but she knew that wasn't even possible. This was extremely upsetting to her.

Luckily, they were interrupted by a food service worker. It was time to eat supper. She brought two trays in. One for Lily, and one for her. "Ma'am," the worker spoke, "We have one celiac-safe gluten-free meal for you. It was a special order by Dr. Thomas. Enjoy!"

Kelly smiled. She was worried they wouldn't know she couldn't eat gluten. *Thank you, Jesus!* She silently prayed for her meal, and she also prayed for her new roommate.

Lord, help this young girl.

Whatever had happened to her must have been traumatic. Trauma was something Kelly knew a little bit about. On the other hand, the girl might not have suffered. Teenage pregnancy seems to happen more and more these days, and she shouldn't be surprised. What alarmed her the most was that she called her baby a *thing.* Normal people don't talk like that. But maybe she wasn't normal. If she had to guess, she'd say she had ADHD or some kind of learning disability. Maybe even a mental handicap.

God, please let me help this poor child.

You Win

Boone woke up early. It wasn't the same without his wife beside him to celebrate their good news. They were not only pregnant again, but they were having two living babies. He prayed they would stay that way.

Just don't take them, Lord.

He knew better than to tell God what to do, but he meant well. All he wanted was a family of his own. It was a dream that had been squashed so many times, it was hard to hope again. But he heard the heartbeats, and everything seemed normal this time.

He worried about her hospital stay, though. Usually, a doctor doesn't admit someone for no good reason. Though he knew the reasons Dr. Thomas explained, his mind still took him everywhere else. All the usual what-ifs rose to the surface again.

Then his cell phone rang, interrupting his thoughts. Thank you, Aunt Sally. Her lovely face was displayed on his phone. His aunt seemed to have perfect timing. He didn't like filling his head with negative scenarios anyway.

"Hello, aunty. I'm sorry I didn't call last night, but it was too late."

"It's never too late, my boy. Don't you know that by now?"

"I know."

The woman was always such a comfort. She levelled him out, just like his mother used to do. They were sisters after all. They were so similar. Whenever he talked to his aunt, he felt like he was talking to his mom again.

"Well…I'm waiting. What did the doctor say?"

"Aunty, I can't tell you on the phone. I need to see you in

person."

"Uh-oh, what's wrong?"

"Nothing is wrong. I just promised Kelly I would talk face to face."

Boone tried very hard not to spill the beans over the phone. He almost did, but a promise is a promise, and if he knew his wife, she'd be very upset if he didn't follow her instructions.

"Isn't Kelly coming over, too?"

"No, she's not here." *Ops, he shouldn't have said that.*

"What do you mean she's not here? Where is she?"

Oh, brother, his aunt was going to dig until she got some answers. "I can't tell you over the phone. I'll be over in about fifteen minutes. Let me get some coffee in me first. It's not even seven o'clock yet. You really can't wait, can you?"

"No, and I haven't slept all night either. I've been praying for you two the whole time."

"Oh...I'm sorry. I appreciate it. I'll come right over, *I promise.*"

"Wait, don't you hang up on me, you little bum."

"Aunt Sally, really. I'm coming over right now." He hung up the phone, smirked, and shook his head. She was impossible sometimes, but he loved her anyway. That's what families do. He was glad he had her as family. She was his second mother and soon-to-be grandmother by proxy to his twins.

What a wonderful thought.

Boone threw oh his clothes, raked his fingers through his red beard to smooth it out, and pulled his long red hair into a ponytail. He had to get it cut soon. It was getting ridiculous. He hadn't gotten it cut since their first miscarriage. It was the Tlingit tradition. Growing his hair and his beard was a way to honour the children he never got to hold. Well, this time, he was meeting his children. He already did an ultrasound.

It was time to let the hair go. It was time to let the pain go.

KNOCK KNOCK KNOCK. Boone rapped on Aunty Sally's door. She looked like a wild woman with her dishevelled salt-and-pepper hair, standing there in her silk housecoat. She looked ready to tar and feather him.

"I know, I know!" He brought her into a hug right away. "I'm sorry. I didn't realize you were so worried."

"Don't ever do that to me again! You guys are all I have."

"Well, that's gonna change pretty quick."

Aunt Sally screamed! "Then it's official?

"It's official! You should have heard their heartbeats! It was incredible!"

"What? *Their* heartbeats?

"WE'RE HAVING TWINS!"

"Oh my Lord in heaven. Are you serious? Two?" Aunt Sally threw her head back and praised the Lord. She started crying and laughing at the same time. Now he knew why she and Kelly got along so well; they were both very emotional.

"I couldn't believe it either. She's already twenty weeks pregnant with the girls."

"GIRLS? Oh, Boone, you're killing me. This is...THE BEST NEWS EVER!"

"We're both overjoyed!"

"So, where's Kelly?

"In the hospital. The doctor is keeping her there for a few days for tests. She had some low vitamin levels, and he wants to make sure everything is okay before she comes home. I think he's being extra careful considering her history."

"Oh my, well, I'm sure she and the babies are in good hands. Now, let me get dressed, and I'll put a pot of coffee on for us. I'm just so tickled pink that the Lord has doubly blessed you guys. Pink, get it?" She laughed.

"Yes, I get it. Now go get some clothes on."

Aunt Sally's excitement was endearing. It really made it feel real. Of course, he knew that it was real, but talking about it really brought it to life. They were having two babies. They were finally having a family of their own. Even though Kelly really pushed to foster kids as an alternative, now they didn't have to. They were getting their own flesh and blood.

That decision to foster didn't come easy either. He

remembered all the night classes they went to shortly after their fourth miscarriage. Boone only did it for Kelly. She hurt so bad, and he just wanted to take her pain away, so he agreed to it.

"I need to hold a child in my arms," she cried. "I don't even care whose it is. I need this, Boone. Please agree with me!"

He was ashamed now at how he behaved. Going through the motions, only to pull the rug out from underneath her once it was approved. His decision to back out still upset her. And after the whole process, he had to go through because of his criminal record. The judge approved him based on his minor theft conviction, stating he posed no threat.

Boone was happy about that, but disappointed in himself when he couldn't go through with it. He took their names off the list against her wishes. Their marriage started to fall apart big time after that. Counselling helped, but he was supposed to work on his control issues. He was supposed to work on a lot of things.

It wasn't just the fostering; it was everything. Boone realized he had to let go and let God. It was hard for him to do. It was hard for him to trust that God had everything under control when all their dreams got crushed over and over again.

Boone couldn't help but feel a sense of relief in this area. God seemed to turn the situation around overnight. Now that they were expecting twins, the tension over fostering seemed to evaporate completely. *Thank you for the healing, God.* What a relief!

Aunt Sally came back to the kitchen fully dressed, talking up a storm. She put a pot of coffee on and sat down. "Before I forget, I wanted to let you know there are some strangers in town. They've been here for the last couple of days. They look pretty shady in my opinion. Four of them. I guess they're renting the old Holloway house up on the ridge. From what I heard from Coffee Row, they came in on two different fishing trawlers. I don't know why they're here, but can you find out?"

"Yah, I'll check it out when I can. I'll be out fishing with my clients all day today and tomorrow, but I'll do some snooping. Maybe they're just here to fish. Don't let your mind get the best of you, Aunt Sally. That's what you always tell me."

"I know, but can you check it out anyway. I don't want to say anything to John at the detachment unless it's really something to worry about."

Boone agreed. The Angoon police department hired him as a part-time peace officer, mostly during the off-season. He took the 15-week Alaska Law Enforcement Training a couple of years ago and has been working with them ever since. The work seemed to suit him well, and it's enjoyable. It was a good supplement to his fishing charter business.

Now, he'd better get going. He had to meet Mr. Romano in an hour and a half.

"Let me cook you some bacon and eggs."

"I really have to go."

"Sit! Let me do this for you. Besides, soon you won't have time to eat. You will be too busy with the twins."

Boone smirked and let the woman dote on him. If his mother were here, she'd do the same thing. After all, he owed her for not calling last night.

"Okay! You win!"

The Bridge

The next morning, Lily had been taken to Antepartum for some tests, and when they brought her back to her room, a social worker was sitting with Lily. She tried to be inconspicuous, but that was hard to do in a room without much privacy. Kelly couldn't help but listen to their conversation.

"Don't mind me," she said. "Just pretend I'm not here."

The social worker looked annoyed and quickly drew the curtain around Lily. It wasn't Kelly's fault they had no privacy. It's not like she had anywhere else to go. She decided to read her emails. After all, they still had a business to run.

"Anyway, as I was saying," the social worker continued, "she won't come. I've explained the situation to her, but she refuses to have anything to do with you or the baby."

"I told you! My mom hates me."

Kelly's heart sank just hearing that. How could any mother hate their child? It was a foreign thing to her. Though Kelly's mom had passed, she knew she loved her. It broke her heart to hear a young girl say that.

"And your father? What about him?"

"I told you, I don't have a father."

Hearing that hurt more than words can say. Kelly remembered saying that as a child. She experienced the same kind of trauma growing up: A father wound. She came from a broken home, and there was nothing that would fix it but Jesus.

Lord, help this girl. Help her find you. Use me if you want.

"If we can't find a relative willing to take you in, you're going to have to go back to the group home, Lily," the social worker told her point-blank.

That's when Lily lost it. "NO! I will not go back there. YOU CAN'T MAKE ME!" she shouted at the top of her lungs.

"Well, actually, we can. You're a minor." Then the social worker stood up, opened the curtain and locked sad eyes with Kelly. She shook her head and left the room.

Lily sat there and cried. "I won't go back there! I won't go back there!"

Kelly let the girl cry without interrupting her or trying to solve her problems. Except for the fact that the two of them seemed to share the same upbringing, she knew nothing more about the girl. What could she possibly say? Yet, something inside of her said, *TRY!*

"Lily? Do you want to talk?"

Then the girl got out of bed and ripped the curtain open. She plopped herself on the side of the bed facing Kelly and rubbed her tear-stained face. "Can I live with you? You're the only person who hasn't treated me like a dog."

Kelly didn't know what to say. The girl was so desperate, she'd ask a total stranger if she could live with them. It was sad. "I'm sure they're just trying to help."

"How, by putting me back in the pound? Do you know what a group home is like? It's like prison. Not like you would know anything about that. You're Miss Perfect."

"Now, that's not fair."

Kelly wanted to defend herself, but she had to remember she was dealing with a child, not an adult. Her brain wasn't even fully developed. Not only that, but she had some sort of mental handicap.

"I'm sorry," the girl cried. "You have your own stuff going on. I forgot."

Well, at least she had empathy. That was a start. *Lord, what do you want me to do here?* The answers were unclear. If the girl needed a listening ear, Kelly could do that, but she couldn't bring her home. Definitely not that.

"I hate to burst your bubble," Kelly told the girl, "but I'm far from perfect. I grew up like you. I didn't have a father. I married an ex-con, and I lost four babies. Like I said, I'm so far from perfect, I don't even know what to call it anymore."

If being vulnerable and exposing her heart didn't do it, nothing would. *Lord, help me.* This is something her therapist told her to work on. *Try.* Just like she heard God tell her to do.

"I have some names to call it. Wanna hear them?"

Kelly giggled. "Not really, but I can imagine." She knew what would help, but it was too soon to broach the subject. Jesus was the father to the fatherless. He had literally saved her life that day; she finally believed with all her heart.

Hopefully, Kelly could share it with her sometime. Right now, the only focus was trust. If Lily trusted her, there was hope. It was the beginning of something. She could tell.

The bridge.

The two of them chatted away. It was odd how well they seemed to understand each other. Kelly realized the girl didn't have a handicap at all. She understood quite well. She just had a hard time dealing with her emotions. *Kind of like her.*

"You're so pretty!" Lily told her. "Not like me."

"Oh, honey, you've got a sweet little face. What do you mean?"

"Yah, you mean these big chubby cheeks and my baggy eyes? Seriously, I look like one of the seven dwarves."

"Don't put yourself down." Kelly used to do that all the time, and it was a hard habit to break. It's part of a father wound. She knew it well. "God made you perfect just the way you are." *Too much too soon,* Kelly thought to herself. But, she might as well see what she says.

"GOD? He didn't have anything to do with making me. Where did you get that from?" The girl became defensive and couldn't let it go. "I doubt there's some big man in the sky making things happen. If there was, then where was he when I needed him? NOWHERE!"

Now Kelly knew what she was dealing with. *An atheist:* Someone mad at God. Now she could move forward. *Let me help her, Jesus!*

"When did you need help, Lily?" Kelly knew it was risky to pry like that, but the door was wide open.

"When I was kicked out. Well, way before that even."

"What happened?"

The girl went on about her abusive stepfather and the violence she witnessed with multiple men her mother dated before him. It was heartbreaking to hear, though the trust she was showing Kelly by exposing her feelings was groundbreaking.

"I'm sorry, sweetheart."

"I hate when people call me that. You're lucky I don't tell you where to go. That name makes me mad. Too many people have called me that and ended up hurting me."

"I'm sorry, I'll call you by your name from now on." Kelly felt another door opening, but she had to open this one very slowly. "Who hurt you, Lily?"

"THE BROTHERS!"

"Who are the brothers?"

"NEVER MIND! I DON'T WANT TO TALK ANYMORE!"

Kelly just sat there as the girl burst into tears. She didn't know if she should go over there and hug her or leave her alone. Something stirred inside of her. *Go to her!* The still, small voice whispered in her head.

"I'm sorry," she told the girl. "I didn't mean to upset you." She wrapped her arms around her and hugged her tightly. Instead of pulling away, Lily held her so tightly she didn't want to let go. It seemed like the poor child was starving for affection.

Oh Lord! What have you gotten me into?

Old Buddy, Old Pal

The weather wasn't cooperating by the time Boone motored to the bay. They were only out for a short time before calling it quits. Not only was it way too foggy to be out safely, but the constant rain didn't make it enjoyable for Mr. Romano and his crew, even though they had their rain gear on.

"We can either try again tomorrow, or I can comp you another couple of days. I'm sorry. Mother Nature has a mind of her own out here."

"It's fine. My wife is tired of fishing anyway. She asked me to take her sightseeing again, and relax before heading back tomorrow. I didn't know how to tell you. You rushed back for us and everything."

"Well, I'm glad you told me. I just want to make sure you guys have a good time while you're here. I hope you come back next summer."

"Oh, don't worry about that. We definitely will. You were awesome."

"I can still take you around the town."

"No, you already did that the first two days. The wife just wants a romantic stroll. Just the two of us. You know how they get."

"I know what you mean."

"Besides, you got your mind on your double surprise. We'll be sure to come back next year to see them. We got three of our own, you know. They're grown now with kids of their own, but I remember how exciting it was when we were first expecting."

The jolly man patted him on the back as they slowly

headed back to the harbour. The rain pelted them as they pulled up their hoods. Boone was glad they were heading back. Kelly and the babies were on his mind. Still, from what the doctor said, she'd be there a couple more days. He'd have to find something else to do.

Aunt Sally's request came to mind.

Boone wondered what these newcomers were doing in Angoon. He saw their boats this morning. Things were pretty quiet around the dock. One of the boats was an old wooden trawler. It didn't look like it had been used to fish for years. Then again, it could be converted into a sightseeing boat. The other boat was a fancy one. It was more like a touring boat. Not a trawler at all. Aunt Sally didn't know the difference, but that was okay.

He supposed he could do some snooping around for the rest of the day. He wouldn't ask anyone at the detachment yet. Boone liked to investigate his own way. He'd head up the hill and just walk around. Usually, he got the feel of something pretty quickly. His guess, they were there to party. A lot of people came to Angoon to get away from the big city. They hear about the little Tlingit town and think it's the perfect place to get away.

It is. That's why he loves it so much.

The town was usually full of tourists from May to September. It was an important part of the economy. He wanted to make sure they weren't chasing away their bread and butter. Without visitors to their town, they wouldn't be a town.

Some came for big game hunting in the fall, and Boone thought maybe they were getting ready for that. The season didn't open until mid-September, though. It wasn't unusual to have guys stay for a few days to get the feel of the terrain first before committing to a hunt. But they still needed a guide, and he was the most experienced. Nobody had contacted him. Not that he'd do it. He had given up on that lifestyle since the last fiasco.

Boone decided he wouldn't guide that part of the island again. They would have to pay him a year's salary before he'd ever consider guiding a hunting party inland. It was too dangerous. He'd stick to fishing, thank you very much.

As the rain continued to pour, Boone headed up to the Halloway house rental. It was an old cabin that the town rented to tourists. Mostly, it remained empty because there were better options, but, in a pinch, it would do if you didn't have a reservation.

Boone walked past the modest log cabin to see if there was anything unusual. He saw lights on and heard laughing. Nothing out of the ordinary. Who could fault a bunch of guys for having fun? Aunt Sally was just being paranoid.

Just to appease her, he decided to knock on the door to welcome them. Hopefully, they would appreciate that and wouldn't see it as being intrusive. Boone lifted his hood and tried not to get wet. The rain was really coming down.

KNOCK KNOCK KNOCK.

Boone stood there for longer than he expected and knocked again. Maybe they didn't hear him. He cupped his hands against the foggy window, hoping to see something. Then, suddenly, the door flew open. "What do you want, buddy?"

A tall, clean-shaven guy with dark hair stood there with his arms crossed. He didn't look very pleased. "Ahem...sorry about that," Boone apologized. "I didn't think you heard me knock. The rain is so loud."

"We heard you, bud. We just ignored you. What do you want?"

Rain pelted him hard as he tried to speak through the thunder. "Can I come in out of the rain for a minute? I just wanted to introduce myself."

Boone figured he'd let them know about Second Chance Charters. At least that way it didn't make him look conspicuous. What would he think if a guy came snooping at his door in the middle of a rainstorm? Nothing good.

The tall man motioned for him to come in. Boone was grateful. "Pleased to meet you," Boone reached out a hand to shake with the gentleman. The man didn't shake it back. He withdrew and cleared his throat. "I run a fishing charter in town. Are you guys interested in that kind of an adventure?"

He could hear a bunch of laughing in the background. "Get rid of him," someone called from another room. Then, they came to join the tall man at the door. They had gang tattoos. Boone spotted that right away. He was well experienced with this kind of crew. Looked like they were all ex-cons. This was not good.

"You got something to say?" A fat older gentleman scoffed.

"Just being a friendly neighbour is all." Boone quickly looked around to get the feel of the place. He saw booze on the table, and what looked like drugs beside it. They had weapons in the corner, and the place smelled like body odour.

"We don't do friendly," another laughed.

Yeah, I know, Boone wanted to say.

The three of them looked like they were going to pound on him. The two without shirts moved forward and flexed their muscles. Boone stepped back immediately. He'd better get out of there before things turned sideways.

"Hey, maybe this dweeb knows something," the smallest in the group announced.

"Shut up, Derek!" The others scolded him.

The tall man with the black hair scratched his nose and made a point of being cordial even after intimidating him. *They wanted something.*

"You happen to know where we can get some women?" The guy winked at him while the others laughed and snickered.

"This isn't that kind of town." Boone locked eyes with him. He knew how to deal with these types of guys. If you didn't stand your ground and show you were the alpha, they would turn into your worst enemy.

"Oh, this isn't that kind of town. Did you hear that?"

"Look, I don't want any trouble," Boone stepped backward toward the door. "I just wanted to welcome you."

"Sure you did. More like you wanted to see what we were

up to. Admit it. You come clean, or we dice you."

And here was the escalation.

Boone would run if he had to, but he'd much rather take a swing at these smug idiots. Instead, he prayed under his breath. *What do I do, Lord?*

When he was in prison, he quickly realized he had to outsmart them. Usually, he played their game long enough to buy himself some time. He pretended to be interested in the same things they were. He could usually turn a situation around if he was clever.

"If you're looking for women, I can probably help you out. You ain't gonna find them here though. Just a bunch of old ladies. You gotta go to Juneau for that." Boone was hoping they'd take the bait.

"Juneau, you say."

"That's right."

"Well, we like 'em young."

Then, someone came down the stairs. He looked like he'd been sleeping. He had a backward ball cap on, bare-chested like the others, littered with tattoos. "We thought you were gonna sleep all day," one of them said. "You finally come down to party, or what?"

"This guy's even gonna hook us up with some ladies," another laughed.

The skinny man dragged his feet to the door and stood beside the tall, black-haired man. He didn't even look up. He just pulled out a revolver and started spinning the chamber to intimidate him. Boone knew this was his cue to exit. He'd run as fast as he could to get help. They'd raid the place before they even knew what happened.

Boone knew better than to walk into this unarmed without backup. Nobody even knew where he was. *Stupid!* Then, Boone stepped backward, holding his hands up. "Just let me go, okay. You'll never see me again."

"What fun would that be?" Someone laughed.

The skinny man came up beside him and pushed him. He

pulled down the hood of his rain jacket, exposing his hair. "And he's a ginger even. You know what they say about gingers. Wait, don't I know you? Yeah, I know you."

"Jimmy?" Boone gulped hard.

"Boys, this guy's one of us. He's an old friend of mine. We did time together, sort of. Just went to different jails. Come on in, old buddy, old pal. We go way back!"

Against Boone's better judgment, he went inside.

The Cult

Boone couldn't get away. It was like he was indoctrinated into their cult. Jimmy kept him there all night long and part of the next day. Kelly would be worried he didn't check in, and Aunt Sally would be furious with him for not calling last night when he said he would.

He felt trapped.

They drank and partied all night. He kept his distance, pretending now and then to drink, sipping on an empty cup. It fooled them enough that they left him alone. They were so drunk they didn't even notice. The drugs apparently were not for them. They were smuggling them. If Boone could just escape, he could get John's team in there and take them down.

But something puzzled him. The fat one they called, Ollie, mentioned it before he passed out. They were looking for someone. A girl. "As soon as we find her, we can get out of here," he said.

Who were they trying to find? Boone tried all night to dig the information out of them. The more he knew, the better. This was a gang of dirtbags. They were going down just as soon as he could figure out what they were up to.

"Join us, Boone dog," Jimmy said. "I work for Sandeep over there. He's the tall guy. I met a buddy of his in prison, and he hooked me up as soon as I got out. You should have seen me, dude, I climbed my way to the top in there. I got a lot of connections now. I make more money than God."

I doubt that, Boone wished he could say.

"So, what kind of business is it?" Boone asked. He knew the answer was something illegal, but he wanted to know what exactly. The more evidence he had to put him away for good, the better.

"We sell goods to the Middle East."

"Seriously? What kind of goods?"

Then Jimmy leaned in close and whispered like he wasn't supposed to tell anyone. "We move human cargo."

Oh, he better not mean what he thinks he means. This was bigger than he thought. If he blows this, it could mean hundreds of lives. "What kind of people? Illegal immigrants?"

"What? No! That wouldn't amount to anything. We move Women. Young ones. We're in charge of the fifteen-and-under group. But keep it quiet. I'm not supposed to broadcast it. I can trust you, though, right, Boone dog?"

"For sure," Boone lied. "He couldn't believe he stumbled upon a human trafficking ring, and his buddy was involved. Ex-buddy that is.

"So, what, you just pick up hookers? How do you get these girls?"

"We take them. Well, not me personally. I mean, we hire all sorts of people to do the dirty work. Men. Women. Old ladies. Housewives. Preachers. We got a pretty big group under us. It's kind of like multi-level marketing."

"Preachers? What do you mean by that?"

"Well, you see those two idiots passed out in the corner? Ollie and his brother Derek? They pretend they're street preachers, and they take the runaways. It's a hoot. They got a good game going. The girls fall for it every time."

Boone wanted to puke. He felt like he was in the lion's den right now.

"So, why come to Angoon?"

"Well, this was the pickup point for one of them. We usually use it because nobody expects it here. They were supposed to be transporting a young girl, but they lost her. Can you believe it? I guess she jumped ship. Probably dead by now, but Sandeep wanted to stay one more day to look. I guess some Saudi prince bought her. He was looking for a specific type. She was a special order. We're all in hot water over it, but we gotta move on. We have some pickups scheduled up and down the coast, all the way to Mexico. Mostly tourist kids. They never watch them. It's pretty easy to snatch 'em. We've got twelve we have to pick up or heads are gonna roll."

Oh, heads were gonna roll all right. Boone was going to make sure of that. All he had to do was get to the detachment. It was already noon, and he still wasn't able to get out of there. Jimmy kept rambling.

"So, you in or what? We can start you with ten grand a month. I know that's not a lot. I make three times that, plus commission, but you can move up the ladder pretty quickly if you know what you're doing. And you're a quick study. I remember that about you. Plus, you're dependable. You got the pipes too. We need guys that can roll heads."

Boone wanted to pretend like he was considering it. "Well, I have my fishing business, can I work for you on the side?"

"Well, that depends. Do people bring their kids on these fishing trips?"

"Sometimes."

"Then, that's perfect. You kidnap the girls, and we'll pay you. All you have to do is text me a picture of her, and I'll give you a date when we can either fly up or boat in. We can do a pickup anytime, except for right now. We're kind of swamped. Like I said, we got twelve to pick up. Business is booming. That means a few days at each port. We can't get back here until, let's see... October probably."

Boone knew if they didn't catch these guys now, it would be too late.

"So, tell me how to start."

"It's simple, catch one. Keep her somewhere safe, and then, like I said, text me her picture. Here's my number. And here's a picture of the girl who jumped ship, too. If you find her, alive, of course, I'll give you 10% of her sale price. And man, that's a good chunk of change if you can bring her in. But yeah, take your time. Like I said, we're backed up until October. Then, when you score your first kid, you're in. That's how it's done. And since you're an ex-con like the rest of us, we trust each other. Trust is the key here, buddy, because if you don't come through…well, let's just say Sandeep is good at his job. There won't be anything left of you. Got it?"

"I got it!"

"Pleasure doing business with you, bud!" They shook hands, and Boone stood to go. He looked at his watch and interrupted the man who was talking about something else now. That's Jimmy, he never stops talking.

Boone headed to the door and escaped in a hurry. He walked until he couldn't see the house anymore, then he started running. He ran so hard that he thought he'd pass out. His stomach churned until he felt the bile rise. He stopped near some bushes and puked his guts out. He wiped his beard and took a breath.

Lord, this is too much!

Watch Your Back

Boone sat there out of breath. He made it to the police detachment, looking over his shoulder the whole time. Hopefully, nobody followed him. If they saw him go into the detachment, he was a goner.

"Are you nuts?" The police chief, John Barlow, asked him after he told him what happened. "We trained you better than that, Boone. You put yourself and your family at risk, and maybe the entire community. Do you realize that if this goes wrong, we may have to put you into the witness protection program? You know what that means."

"I'm sorry," Boone told him, feeling defeated. "I had no choice. I was trapped. I didn't see any other option."

"Well, now you gotta see this through to the end."

"I plan to."

"How? How do you plan to do that, wise guy?"

It was embarrassing. Not only did Boone get himself in way over his head, but he didn't even have a plan. How was he supposed to pull this off?

"We have some time to investigate them, don't we? Then, I can contact them and say I got a kid for them. I can wear a wire. I'll do whatever it takes."

"You don't know who you're dealing with here. These guys are professionals."

Boone wanted to tell him Jimmy was no professional, but he didn't think going into their history would be helpful. Besides, all John needed to know was that he knew one of them. Sure, he knew about Boone's incarceration, but not that Jimmy was the guy who caused it. It was ancient history.

"I thought you told me you had to take a picture of the girl."

"I did. Can't we fudge that, though? I can send them a fake."

"Like I said, they are professionals. You don't think they'll know?"

"Yah, you got a point."

John rubbed his head. His frustration was obvious. "Let me do some digging. We'll have to come up with a plan. Sounds like we've got time on our side, and that means we'll be ready for them. You'd better pray that whatever plan we come up with is a good one, or you can kiss your life goodbye. They'll make sure of that. I mean it, Boone! And don't tell anyone what happened here. Just you and me. Keep it between us. At least until we come up with a solid plan."

"I can tell Kelly, right?"

"No, you can't. You can't tell a soul until I say so. Even then, it's only the detachment that will know, and just a select few of them. I'll have to get a team ready."

"John, seriously! I can't keep this from my wife."

"Well, you're going to have to. It's too risky for her to know."

Boone pressed his palm against his headache; it was throbbing so hard he couldn't see straight. How was he supposed to hide this from Kelly? She usually saw right through him. Especially right now with the babies coming. She'll know something's up.

"Can't we just go over there now and arrest them? Save us the trouble of planning all this out? They're right there. I'll testify to what I was told."

"We can't arrest them. They haven't done anything yet."

"What do you mean? They're also smuggling drugs. I saw it. They told me."

John scratched his head. Boone could tell he was thinking about it. It would be better for everyone if they just went and arrested them now.

"Well, either we get them on drug charges, or we go for the big fish. And trust me, there are bigger fish involved. You have no idea what you've stumbled upon. These guys are the bottom end of the totem pole. I want the big ones at the top, every single one of them. We gotta protect our kids. These guys need to go down!"

"I see your point. I want these dirtbags, too."

Boone knew he was in for a hard ride. It would be difficult, but he'd have to keep Kelly out of it for her protection. That meant he couldn't tell her a thing. Hopefully, she'd be too focused on the babies to notice he had other things on his mind.

God, I need you to help me with this. Keep my family safe.

"Do you think it's wise to send a squad car to the Halloway house right now? Or, do you think that'll just make them think you're on to them? It might even make them think I was a snitch. I know what these kinds of guys do to snitches, and it ain't pretty."

"No, we won't risk your life, Boone. Trust me on that one. I don't want them thinking you snitched on them. If they have any suspicions at all, they won't even come back. As ugly as it is, we need them to come back here. We need to catch them red-handed."

Boone breathed a sigh of relief. At first, he wanted the police to arrest them right then, but John was right. They had to wait, or the whole thing would be blown, including his cover. He'd have to take his cue from John and the team he put on this. They would have to come up with a clever plan, or he would be in trouble.

There's no way Boone wanted to go into witness protection. They would have to leave everything they worked so hard to build here in Angoon. They would have to leave Aunt Sally. They would have to leave all their friends. This place. Their culture. Their history. Their future. That was not going to happen if he could help it.

Boone had to do some serious praying. This wasn't going away overnight. He had to think. He had to figure out how he was going to pull this off without anyone knowing what he was up to. He would never kidnap a child, yet that's what he signed up for.

How on earth was this going to work?

"So, we're clear then, Boone?" John asked him as he nodded. "You leave this up to us, do you hear me? Once we come up with a plan, we'll schedule a meeting with you. Don't do anything out of the ordinary, and especially stay away from the Halloway house today."

"I don't plan to go back there."

"Good! I'll have a couple of guys do surveillance of the dock. We'll watch when they leave, and then I'll get to work on a plan."

Boone nodded. It was time for him to go home. He'd sneak out the way he came and make sure nobody saw him there.

"And Boone?" John added.

"Yah?"

"Watch your back!"

I Don't Know How

K elly was finally going home. As long as her numbers were up today, she was told she didn't have to return for two weeks. They had completed all the necessary tests, and the girls were fine, and so was she.

Boone still wasn't answering, though. She'd tried all evening, and now this morning. Still no answer. She even tried Aunt Sally, and she was fuming mad that Boone didn't check in with her yet. This was not like him at all. Perhaps he got carried away fishing with his clients. She hoped that's all it was.

Still, it made her worry, though that was the last thing she was supposed to be doing. Aunt Sally told her so when she called her. She knew it wasn't going to change the situation, and it would only put the babies at risk. She definitely didn't want to do that. Instead, she kept on praying. *Lord, watch over Boone, whatever he's doing. Something's wrong!*

Just then, Lily came back crying with the social worker. "You can't take him! I DIDN'T GIVE YOU PERMISSION! I know my rights!"

The social worker flew up her hands and said, "I'll be back when you calm down."

Kelly wondered what was happening, and then decided to get up and close the door so she could talk to the girl. She trusted her and hoped she would open up. "What's wrong, Lily?"

The girl just bawled.

Kelly sat beside her on her bed and held her hand. "You know I'm here for you. What's happening? Maybe I can help."

"You can't help. You said I can't live with you. So, who cares!"

"Lily, don't be like that. I said, I would if I could. Maybe I can help in other ways?"

Kelly could see that the girl's hormones were playing a big part in her emotional state. She knew how that was. With all her miscarriages, she experienced uncontrollable highs and lows.

Lily started pulling at her hair and screaming through tears.

I need help here, God! Please!

Kelly decided to hum a hymn. The girl didn't know it, but that didn't matter. She held her hand and began to hum the tune, *Just as I am.* It was a lovely hymn that always seemed to settle her down during her most difficult times. Maybe it would help Lily.

The girl dropped her head onto Kelly's shoulder. She cried softly until she finally calmed down. Kelly reminded herself that this girl was just a child. She needed a mother. She needed someone to care. She needed *her.*

Kelly knew she shouldn't get so emotionally attached to her, but she couldn't help it. "Now, take a breath and tell me what is happening. Why are you so upset?"

"They said they are taking my baby into protective services today."

"But, didn't you say you didn't want him?"

Lily lifted her head and withdrew. "I SAID I DON'T KNOW!" she barked.

"It's okay to change your mind, sweetheart. I'm sorry, I mean Lily."

The teenager looked at her sideways. "You better be!"

Kelly sighed; she didn't want to get on the girls' bad side. This talk was crucial. It might be the last time she ever gets a chance to tell her about Jesus. *How Lord? How do I tell her without upsetting her? Is now even the right time?* She took a deep breath and waited for the Lord to answer. In her spirit, she could feel the answer come. *Live it!*

And so I will. I will love her like you do, Jesus. Kelly decided instead of trying to push anything on the girl, she'd just listen. She'd talk to her with a heart of compassion, instead of using accusative language. She tried another way.

"Did you see the baby yet?"

"NO!" Lily shouted.

Outbursts usually meant strong emotions one way or the other, so Kelly decided to ask her, "Do you want to see him, Lilly?"

The girl started to cry. *Of course she did. She just didn't know how to say it.*

"Why don't I try to see if we can get him brought to the room?"

"You could do that?"

"I don't see why not."

Kelly smiled and stood up. "You just leave it to me. I can be very persuasive when I want to be." What the girl needed most was her mother. She wasn't her mother, but she could act like it in this instance. She needed someone to fight for her. If she couldn't give her anything else, at least she could give her that.

The hallway was busy, but Kelly knew what to do. She'd had a lot of experience in hospitals as a patient and an employee. Someone had to be at the nursing station. Great! It was the bully nurse from before. She was the only one on. Better than nothing. "Excuse me," Kelly interrupted her phone conversation, "I need to speak with you."

If there was one thing Kelly learnt from everything she'd been through in the last few years, it was how to speak up for herself. She used to be a people pleaser. She was still a little, but Boone helped her learn. He was a great teacher. *So was God!*

"Wha'd ya want?"

"That young lady in there has not seen her baby yet. She would like to immediately!"

The nurse hung up the phone and glared at her. "You're not her mother, so what do you think you're doing? You think you're helping? Well, you're not. You're just making it harder. She's putting the kid up for adoption. We don't recommend her seeing it."

"First, it's not an it! Second, she didn't sign any papers

yet, so why is protective services taking her baby today?" Kelly shook. She needed to calm down. Confrontations were still hard.

The old nurse sighed. "Fine! Maybe later this afternoon."

"No, NOW!"

If Kelly had to go get the baby herself, she would. Though there was no legal way she could make that happen. Maybe if she walked Lily to the nursery, they would let them take the baby back to the room. Why not? She's the mother.

"Lady, mind your own business! I said, Maybe later! Now, don't tell me how to do my job!"

Then do your job! Kelly wanted to say.

She decided against arguing with the woman because getting upset wasn't worth it. Boone taught her that. No, she had another plan. She shook her head at the lady and headed back to her room. Thankfully, the mean woman darted off in the opposite direction. Now would be the time to implement her plan.

As soon as she got back to the room, she said, "C'mon, Lily! We're going to get your baby." Her adrenaline was pumping, and for a moment, she wondered if it would be good for the twins. *Lord, help me!*

"We can do that?"

"Of course, we can do that. Well, *you* can do that. I'm just helping." Kelly looked around as the two of them escaped down the hallway. Kelly had seen it several times, just not from the inside.

When they got to the doorway, Kelly whispered, "Tell them you want to see your baby. I'm not allowed in there, but you can go get him, and we'll bring him back to the room."

"I can't do it by myself."

"Yes, you can!" Kelly rested a hand on her shoulder. "You're stronger than you think!"

Kelly watched that girl slowly shuffle toward a nurse inside the nursery. She looked back at her and gave her a nod. Then a nurse stopped beside Lily and they talked. It was hard to make out what they were saying, but they kept looking over at her. Then Lily motioned for Kelly to come join her.

Smart girl!

Lily locked arms with Kelly. She could feel the girl's body shaking. Poor thing. She couldn't imagine how hard this must be for a teenage mother. Miscarriage was hard enough, but this was a whole other kind of pain. No wonder she convinced the nurse to let her come in with her.

"Now, this one's yours," the kind nurse smiled at Lily. "Someone's been waiting for you to come say hi to him. He's got a good set of lungs. We've given him formula for now, but depending on what you decide...well, you know all that. "I'll leave you guys alone for a moment. Just give me a shout if you need me."

Kelly couldn't believe how easy it was. All they had to do was check that Lily's bracelet matched the baby's. She fought off tears as she looked around. It brought back painful memories of her losses, yet, at the same time, gave her hope for the twins inside of her. Looking at Lily now, struck her emotionally. She could feel both pain and joy at the same time.

"Hi, little guy," the girl whispered. She touched the baby's hand, and he grabbed onto her finger. "You see that? He knows me!"

"Of course, he knows you! You're his mother."

"I'm his mother," she choked up.

"Do you want to hold him?" Kelly asked, hoping she wasn't overstepping.

Lilly nodded and dried her tears. "Don't we need the nurse?"

"Nope, just pick him up."

"I don't know how."

Lily was shaking as she fought off more tears. Kelly realized she may need some guidance. "I'll help you." She leaned over and scooped up the tiny newborn into her arms. It felt good to hold a child. Oh, how she longed for this. *Lord, me!*

Lily watched her as she instructed how to support the head and hold the child. She transferred the baby to Lily, as she cautiously adjusted her arms to cradle him. It was a tender moment, even for the nurse who was watching from across the room.

"He's so small. What if I hurt him?"

"You won't."

The nurse brought a chair for both of them, and they sat for a while with the baby. Lily was quiet most of the time as she looked at the little guy's sweet face. He was a miracle. All children are, no matter the circumstance. It's God's blessing. Of course, Lily didn't know that yet, but she was beginning to understand.

Lily began to hum like Kelly had done to her. It wasn't the same tune, but it was her own version. It was tender and endearing. The girl cared for the child after all. They were making a bond, and that was a good thing.

When it was time to go, Lily set the baby back down in the isolette and tucked him in like a doll. They were getting ready to go when he started wailing loudly.

"I told you he's got some good pipes," the nurse said as she came over. "Looks like the little one wants to stay with his mommy. You can take him to your room, you know."

Lily looked at Kelly, and Kelly nodded. "It's okay. I can help you."

The two of them rolled him out of the nursery and down the hall to their room. It was complete bliss. Kelly breathed a sigh of relief as tears welled in her eyes. It was time to call Boone so he could get her out of there.

Her job was done!

The Stunt

By the time Kelly got hold of Boone, it was already well into the afternoon. She gave him heck for not answering his calls, but he said he'd explain when he got there. He told her he was jumping on a plane right away to come pick her up. She knew that meant he wouldn't be there for several hours. She was ready to go home now, though she loved holding Lily's baby. She was happy the girl was finally bonding with her newborn. Maybe they had a chance after all. If she had the proper support, she would be a good mother.

Several nurses were in and out of their room all afternoon, helping her learn how to change and feed the baby. It was enjoyable to be part of that, though Kelly knew at some point, she'd have to say goodbye. It worried her that the social worker was not pleased that she had the baby in her room. She said she'd be back later, but hoped she'd stay away. Her presence made Lily nervous, and that didn't help the situation.

"I thought you were going home," Lily asked her after laying the sleeping baby down. She just fed her a bottle and lay down to rest."

"I am, but my husband has been busy with clients." I have to wait for him to fly in to get me. We'll probably end up staying in Juneau for the night. I doubt he'll make it here before dark, and I definitely don't want to fly after dark. I'm kind of skittish when it comes to flying. I've had some bad experiences."

"I don't like boats," Lily told her. "I had a bad experience too."

"You did? Like what?"

Lily closed her eyes and shook her head. "You don't want

to know."

"I'll share my story if you share yours," Kelly giggled.

"We're a lot alike, you know," Lily said. "I wish you were my mother. I even look like you. Blonde hair, blue eyes. Or, we could be sisters. I never had a sister. I wish I could go home with you."

Kelly knew where she was going with this. She kept trying to get her to change her mind. It's not like she didn't want to. She really did. They were all set up to do foster care, but Boone pulled the rug out from under it. Without his support, it wouldn't work.

"I know. We could keep in touch," Kelly told her. She knew that wasn't the same, but it was all she had. Boone would never change his mind. It was hopeless. It was the source of tension for quite a while between the two of them. Too many fights. Too much pain.

And now, with the pregnancy, the situation had turned around. God turned it around for them. She didn't need to foster children when she could have her own. Yet, something gnawed at her. This girl needed a home. If only Boone would change his mind. *God, what do you want? It's not about what we want. If there's a way to help Lily, please find it before I go home.*

The door opened suddenly, interrupting Kelly's silent prayer. It was the social worker with the mean charge nurse. *Uh-oh, something was up.* By the looks on their faces, this did not look good.

"Lily, we've come for the baby."

"What do you mean you've come for the baby?" Kelly snapped.

"Stay out of it, Mrs. McKenzie! This is none of your business!" The nurse told her as the social worker went to grab the newborn.

"NO! I AM KEEPING MY BABY!"

"You can't make her give up her baby!" Kelly defended her. "She's the mother! She's got rights! You can't do this!"

Lily stood up and pulled on the baby's bed. "Nurse! Please

hold her back! She is a danger to that child and a danger to others."

The big nurse held Lily in place as another came running into the room to help her. They pushed her down on her bed and held her there, one taking one arm and another taking the other.

"This isn't right!" Kelly stood up.

"Mrs. McKenzie, we are not telling you again! SIT DOWN!"

"NO!" Kelly fumed.

"Get security!" The charge nurse told another nurse standing in the doorway.

Kelly was infuriated. They were browbeating this poor teenager into giving up her child. "I'm going to get security myself if you don't take your hands off this poor child. I know the law too, and you can't do this. The police chief in Angoon is a pretty good friend of mine. All I have to do is call him, and he'll have the Juneau police at your doorstep. Not only that, but my husband's a peace officer for them, and he'll be here soon."

Lily was screaming, struggling to free her arms as the baby wailed. They weren't budging. They continued to hold Lily down as hospital security came running. Kelly shook her head and folded her arms in front of her. She wasn't budging either.

"Ma'am, you're going to have to come with us."

"No! I'm not going anywhere! I know my rights. I did nothing wrong." Kelly trembled.

"Let's everyone just take it down a notch, then," the officer tried to defuse the situation. "You! Sit!" He pointed to her. "You! Stop crying!" He pointed to Lily. "And somebody please pick that crying baby up before he chokes."

The social worker reached into the isolette and grabbed the baby. She rocked him and settled him, and put a soother in his mouth. "Now please," she jiggled the newborn, talking in a calm voice. Much better than before. "Let me explain. Everyone just listen."

The security officers stood on guard, and the nurses continued to hold Lily in place so she couldn't get out of her bed. Kelly sat and listened too. They'd better explain properly, or this wasn't going to end well.

"Lily is a minor; so is the baby. Unless we have foster care for both of them at the same foster facility, we can't keep them together. Right now, we only have foster care for the baby. Lily has to go back to the group home she ran away from. They are not equipped to take a newborn. I'm sorry, that's the way it is."

"NOO!" Lily cried, "YOU CAN'T MAKE ME!"

Kelly wanted to scream. That poor child. Her hands were tied. It seemed barbaric to separate a mother from her baby. Was this really the only option?

Lily started hyperventilating. She held her breath until her face went blue, then burst out crying and gagging. It was a horrible sight to see. She screamed like they were murdering her. If there was anything Kelly could do, it was to help her calm down. She decided to use what Boone had taught her in dealing with her emotions. Calm, deep breaths. Kelly struggled with panic attacks long enough to know what to do.

"Lily, you're okay!" she spoke directly to her. "Can you guys bring her over here to my bed? Just for a second?"

They did as she asked, realizing her voice alone had started to calm the teenager down. She hummed the same hymn and soothed her like before. She wrapped her arms around the girl as she continued to hum. "It will be okay, Lily. I will take you and the baby home with me."

Before she realized what had popped out of her mouth, she couldn't take it back. The entire traumatic experience had forced her hand. This had to happen. There was no other way.

"Oh no, you're not, Mrs. McKenzie. We can't just let anyone take a child or a newborn home unless you're related. It's not legal," the social worker said.

"I am a legal foster parent. I can and I will."

The social worker whispered with the nurses and security, then came back to her and Lily on the bed. "I'm really hoping you can prove this."

"I can prove it! We'll take her home tonight. My husband's on his way. Just ask Dr. Thomas. He knows us. I'm sure he'll vouch for us."

"We need more than that," the social worker said. She set the quiet infant back down in its bed. "I will run your name through the system, then we'll talk. She left the room immediately, and the rest of the staff followed her.

Lily got up and grabbed the baby, then came back to sit with Kelly. "Thank you!" She told her. "I love you!"

Kelly bit her lip and hugged her. Either she just did something really good, or really stupid. If Boone didn't give his consent, it would all be over for the girl. *Jesus! Please change Boone's mind! We need a miracle here.*

He could very well divorce her for a stunt like this.

Not In a Million Years

It was terrible that he got in so late. It was already getting dark. Boone was ashamed it took him this long to get there. Not only did he miss his original flight, but he had to pay a lot of money for a special charter.

He was losing control.

Boone knew this was not going to end well. His wife was already upset with him for not answering his phone. What on earth was he going to tell her? This was already getting out of hand. He wondered if he should just come clean and tell her everything. But then, that would be going against a direct order, and he knew better than that. John was right; if he said anything, he'd be putting her in danger.

He knew the kind of men he was dealing with. He knew what they were capable of. Most of all, he knew what Jimmy was capable of, or at least he assumed. When Boone knew him, he was already pretty bad, but now, after years in prison, he was much worse. Not only that, he added murder to his repertoire while he was there. That's why his sentence was extended.

Boone hurried into the hospital and went straight to his wife's room. "Where is she? He asked the nurse at the desk after seeing an empty room.

"Who?"

"Kelly McKenzie."

"Oh, she's in the nursery with the baby. They're ready to go."

"What? No, my wife is still pregnant…isn't she?"

The nurse looked confused. She must be new. She probably got her confused with someone else. Kelly was only five months pregnant. She couldn't have the baby this early, could she? Panic hit Boone suddenly. What was going on?

"Oh, hello there, Boone," Dr. Thomas said, bumping into him in the hallway. "I hoped I would still be here when you arrived. I was just heading home." He looked at his watch and smiled. "A little late, are we?"

"I know, I know," Boone cringed. "Long story."

"Well, I'm sure it's a good one," he grinned. "Anyway, I just wanted to tell you your wife is doing wonderful. I'd like to see her in a couple of weeks. Looks like the two of you are in for some sleepless nights. I made sure you have enough diapers and a car seat, since you won't be heading home until tomorrow morning. After that, just bring the baby in when Kelly comes in for her next checkup."

What on earth?

Boone pretended to know what was going on, but really, he didn't have a clue. Did she have the baby already? He wasn't thinking clearly. Was that even possible?

"Sounds good, doc."

As soon as Dr. Thomas turned the corner, Boone was off like lightning. "Where's the nursery?" He asked the first nurse he bumped into. This was crazy.

"Oh, down the hall and to your left," the nurse pointed.

Boone hurried as fast as he could, passed the elevator, passed the cleaning cart, and passed the vending machine. He gulped as he ran, trying to prepare himself for whatever this was.

Finally, he reached the doors of the nursery and panted out of breath.

"There you are!" His wife headed over. "What took you so long?"

Boone couldn't speak. He just stood there, puzzled.

"What's the matter?"

"I-um, are you okay?"

Kelly leaned in and kissed him. "Yes, silly, the doctor gave me a clean bill of health. You look like you've seen a ghost. Do you need to sit down?"

Boone shook his head and wiped his brow. He realized he must have worked things up in his mind. It was crazy what he was thinking. He didn't even want to say it out loud.

Then, Boone watched as the nurse came over with a baby in her arms. She gave it to Kelly. "All cleaned up. This little one is ready to go home."

Boone trembled. "What? Whose baby is this?"

Kelly ignored him and introduced him to the nurse instead. "Oh, this is my husband, Boone. He's the guy we've been waiting for all day," she winked.

Boone shook her hand and stood there with his mouth open.

"Now, his car seat is over there by the door. I've stocked the diaper bag as per the doctor's notes, and everything is set to go."

"Where's Lily?" Kelly spun around, looking for someone. None of it made sense, but Boone decided not to make a scene. He'd ask his wife in private as soon as the nurse left.

"She went to the bathroom. She needed my help, but she should be out soon."

Then the nurse left and went back to her station. He stood beside his wife and, apparently, a newborn baby they were taking home. Boone couldn't even begin to put the pieces together properly. This was insane.

"What on earth is going on?" he whispered sideways.

"Just go along with me," she whispered back. "I need this, Boone."

Boone was starting to boil. It was beginning to make sense. "She had agreed to take this baby home without his consent. She knew how he felt about fostering. This was not happening. Over his dead body. "NO!" Boone said louder than he intended.

"Boone, please! Don't make a scene." She turned and walked to the corner, where it was more private. "We're fostering this child. I can explain everything later. Right now, I need you to pretend you knew about it and sign some papers with the social worker on the way out, or everything will fall apart."

"No! That's not gonna happen, and you know why."

"Honestly, Boone, I'm not arguing with you here. For once, just let me take the lead. I can explain everything later, and I'm sorry I didn't ask you first, but this child needs us right now, and so does his mother."

"His mother?" What kind of ridiculousness was going on here?

Then, Kelly turned nervously and headed over to someone who was headed toward them. A short, round young girl shuffled toward her. She stopped to whisper something, and then the two of them came over to Boone. Kelly still cradled the baby in her arms, shifting her weight with it as she walked.

"Cool, man," the elfin-faced girl spoke to him in a childlike voice. She looked oddly familiar. "Love the tattoos. You get those in prison or what?"

He turned to Kelly and grinned through his teeth. *Don't make a scene, Boone. Go along with this, Boone.* He could hear his wife's voice drilled in his head. The only problem was, he was NOT going to go along with whatever this craziness was. Not on your life.

"Kelly, give the baby back to her mother."

"Why?" Kelly looked alarmed. She reluctantly transferred the baby back to its rightful owner.

"Uh-oh," the girl said, "Trouble in paradise. I'll go sit down."

The nurse suddenly came over, realizing something was up. "Is everything okay over here? Aren't you guys headed over to the social worker? She's waiting for you."

"We are," Kelly told her. "Lily, I'll be right back. I just need to talk to my husband in the hallway first."

Boone stood there with his arms crossed. He looked at the girl's funny face. She seemed handicapped. He had seen her somewhere before. It was the oddest thing. Why couldn't he remember where he knew her from?

He didn't appreciate his wife bamboozling him into this. He was adamant about not doing foster care. How could she go against his back like this? Especially now with them expecting. *Lord, give me strength. Help me to knock some sense into her.* There was no way this was going to happen.

Not in a million years!

The Fight

Boone pulled them into a maintenance closet in the hospital hallway and shut the door. He turned on the light and looked at his wife's tear-stained face. He had to tread softly. He knew how much she wanted a baby, and thought having her own would take away the urge to foster, but apparently it hadn't. This was outright betrayal.

Breathe, Boone! Calm down and take it slow.

"Why didn't you ask me?"

"I tried phoning you for two days. Where were you, Boone? You better not be cheating on me, because it'll be the last thing you ever do!"

"Cheating? No! I would never!"

Boone knew she was extra sensitive to that because of her previous boyfriend's philandering ways, but not him. That wasn't what he was about.

"You never called me. You just left me there."

"I didn't leave you," he sighed. He knew she had abandonment issues because her father left her when she was a child, but this was over the top. Her pregnancy hormones must be getting the best of her.

"I shared a room with Lily. She's been through a lot, and they were going to separate her from her baby if they couldn't find foster care for both of them at the same place. It was a last-minute thing. I didn't even have time to ask you."

"Why are you the only one who can solve people's problems? You have a hero complex, you know that! It doesn't always have to be you who saves the day, you know. Let someone else fix it for once."

"Who? You weren't there. You didn't see her pain when they tried to take her baby away from her. Boone, she begged me to take her home with me. Do you know what that did to my heart? And then when I saw her sweet newborn's face…I couldn't say no."

"WELL, I CAN!"

Boone didn't want to be the bad guy here, but someone had to. It wasn't even realistic. How were they supposed to take care of a handicapped teenager and a newborn baby at the same time? Not to mention running a business, a high-risk twin pregnancy, and his situation with Jimmy and the police.

At the same time, his communication skills were lacking here, too. The secret he carried was just as crazy as hers. They both needed help. Maybe they should head back to their therapist on Monday, considering how this has impacted their marriage again. Boone thought it had been dealt with, but not anymore. It was the same argument all over again, just in different ways. This time topped it all.

"Boone, don't do this to me! Not again. I need you to sign the papers. The social worker is waiting for us in her office. The only thing left is for you to give your okay. If you don't, they will take her baby from her tonight, and she'll never see him again."

"I'm sure she'll see him again. Come on, quit catastrophizing. Why do you always do that? I'm sure social services can handle everything just fine without you."

"You don't understand," Kelly bawled.

"Look, my main concern is that you and the babies are okay. That's all I care about. We're not responsible for every stray that comes along."

Just as he said that, he realized that wasn't the right word. He knew what he meant, but it came out wrong, and Kelly reacted immediately. She pushed him away and told him she was done. Boone hoped she was just upset and didn't mean to be done with the marriage. He always seemed to put his foot in his mouth lately.

"I'll be in the social worker's office. If you have a heart, be there in five minutes. It's at the end of the hall and around the corner." She slammed the door hard and stormed off the way she came. Boone just stood there, stunned.

Lord, I need a little help. She's impossible.

At this point, he didn't know what to do. They were at a stalemate. If he didn't meet her in the social worker's office, their marriage was done. If he did sign the papers, they'd be at odds with each other, and likely it would be the end of them anyway.

All Boone knew was that his bladder was calling. He had to find a bathroom soon before he did anything else. Then he would decide. He went down several hallways before he finally found a public washroom.

The argument reeled in his mind. He second-guessed himself and his choice of words, his attitude about it, and how he came across to her. *Am I wrong?* It didn't make sense to sign the papers. Why should he have to commit to a silly predicament like this? It wasn't his fault, or Kelly's. It was that stupid teenager's fault for getting herself pregnant. Why don't her own parents help?

Boone dried his hands and then shoved them into his pockets. He remembered he still had that picture Jimmy gave him. It was the girl they were looking for. Boone pulled it out and looked at it again. *What?* He looked at it closely. *It was her!* The girl in the photo was the same handicapped girl in the nursery: The mother of the child Kelly wanted to foster. He was sure of it. Same elfin face. Same chubby cheeks. Same blonde hair and blue eyes.

Panic hit him hard. He shoved the picture back in his pocket and stood there in shock. He didn't know what to think. If she was the same girl Jimmy and his thugs were looking for, that meant they had abducted her.

This changes everything.

Boone looked at his watch. It had been well over fifteen minutes since he and Kelly had it out in the closet. He knew by now, his wife would be furious. But maybe there was still a chance. He flew out of the bathroom and ran down the hall to where she said the social worker's office was.

She wasn't even there.

"Can I help you?" The lady inside asked him. She lowered her reading glasses and shuffled some paperwork on her desk.

"I-um, I'm looking for my wife. I was supposed to sign some papers?"

"Oh yes, you must be the husband. Sit."

Boone entered the room and sat down. He wondered where Kelly was. He looked around, but she hadn't arrived. *Come on, Kells-Bells, you're killing me!*

"I'm sure Mrs. McKenzie filled you in."

Boone wanted to roll his eyes. *I wish!* Instead, he just nodded.

"I have everything ready for you to sign." She pointed out the spots for him to initial and sign. It was like signing his life away.

"Do you know where the girl's parents are?" He asked.

"The mother and stepfather refused to take her back. She was sent to a special needs group home after running away. Then, she ran away from the group home, and then she disappeared for a while. She turned up at the old lighthouse in Angoon. I'm sure you would be familiar with that place since you're from there."

"Sure, I know the place." Boone knew why she had disappeared, but he wasn't about to say anything to the woman. It would blow the whole thing if she started to question how he knew.

"We figure she met a boy there and, well... you know the rest of the story. We see this kind of thing all the time. It's unfortunate. We're hoping for reconciliation between Lily and her mother, but not sure if that will happen. We'll have weekly visits with her at your home, and it's important to keep us updated on her progress. She is a special needs case, and we're not sure about the infant yet. Are you prepared to do this, Mr. McKenzie?

"Yes, I am."

"Well, good, because you come highly recommended by Dr. Thomas despite your sordid past. But we understand you have a pardon, and you were approved quite easily. That said, we will still be monitoring you and making sure all the needs of both minors are met accordingly.

"I understand."

"And lastly, though you've been through all the classes and I'm told you and your wife are fully prepared, this is your first foster, and it's a big one. If you need support in any way, please reach out and let us know what those needs are. We've got quite a robust support system for foster parents here, especially new ones."

Boone took a breath. He got up from his seat, shook the woman's hand and turned around to see his wife. He hadn't realized she was standing at the doorway the whole time. She stood there like a mother hen, car seat and baby in hand, with an arm around the teenager. "Let's go home," he said.

The new blended family trailed slowly down the hall and out of the hospital. He knew they weren't making it home tonight. He called a cab that took him to one of Juneau's best hotels. He got a double room so Lily could have privacy and Kelly could go back and forth between them to help with the baby.

"I'm sorry, Boone," Kelly whispered in the quiet of the night as they lay there. Lily and the baby were finally asleep.

"I'm sorry too, Kells. Let's go see the therapist again. I think we need it."

"Okay."

Boone kissed his wife, and then he kissed her belly. His children were still safe inside her womb. That was an accomplishment in itself. All he had to do was make sure predators like Jimmy were never a threat to his own girls.

He would make sure of that!

Jesus, I'm sorry about how I behaved. Please help Lily and the baby be okay. Help the police force come up with a plan that doesn't include risking his family's life.

Boone wished he could tell his wife about everything. It

hung over him like a heavy cloud. He'd have to skirt around it somehow and pretend everything was fine. Even if he couldn't tell her the truth, he knew keeping it from her was the right thing to do. Her safety depended on it. So did the others.

Five lives hung in the balance. Six, if you counted him.

He could not blow this!

Sleep

Morning came early with a baby in the house. Night ran into day and day ran into night. It got to a point where Kelly didn't even know what day it was. Even though she included Lily in the infant's care as much as possible, the girl was still a child herself. Full responsibility rested solely on Kelly.

Boone was preoccupied with the business and spent the better part of the fall chartering new fishing tours. They were very busy and very grateful for the extra income due to the warm weather. Kelly hadn't seen such a warm, sunny fall in a long time. Usually, the weather in Angoon, Alaska, was temperamental and rainy this late in the season.

"What a beautiful day! I can't believe it's November already," Lily smiled as she cleaned up the kitchen. The girl had been doing great since arriving. Not only had she learned how to help with the day-to-day childcare for her baby, but she also took a real interest in him. The first few weeks were difficult, but once she recuperated from the birth trauma she went through, things started to look up.

Lily's Williams Syndrome diagnosis seemed to improve. Kelly was told the girl had suffered from it since birth, but from the research she found, she realized it was associated with celiac disease. It was a blessing that their household was a designated gluten-free zone, because Lily had no choice but to eat what they ate.

It was like she was a whole new girl. Kelly even had them run a celiac blood panel on Lily as soon as she figured out the girl might have what she has. It turned out that she was positive. What were the odds? God sure had a sense of humour. He knew she needed to be with them. That's why He brought her into their lives. Even Boone seemed happy with the arrangement, though he seemed preoccupied with his peace officer duties. He was gearing up for the winter months when he switched employment to law enforcement.

Kelly could tell he was working hard with John to keep Angoon safe. They had meetings twice a week. Not much happened in their little town, but it was always good to be cautious. Soon, the twins would be born, and she felt blessed to raise them in such a safe community. Aunt Sally commented on that the other day. It was a nice place to raise her grandchildren.

"Did you hear me?" Lily asked as she washed the dishes. "I said it's another beautiful day. I think we should take Charlie out for a walk. What do you think, Kelly? Or are you too tired again? Your baby bump is getting huge. I wish I had known I was pregnant. I thought I was just fat."

The girl jabbered away as Kelly realized she was talking to her. She fazed out at the kitchen table again, exhausted as usual. Even though she was thankful for the tea Lily had made her, she could barely keep her eyes open. The twins kept her up all night kicking her ribs, and then she had to feed Charlie twice.

"Oh, I'm sorry, Lily, I'm not much company, am I?" she said as she cradled the warm cup in her hands. At this point, she was tired of being tired and achy. She only had a few more weeks to go. Dr. Thomas said if the twins keep growing at the rate they are, they might induce her at 36 weeks. Kelly wished it were right now. Her ribs and back ached so badly, nothing seemed to relieve the pain.

Lily dried her hands and pulled up a chair. "I can call Aunt Sally if you want. She told me yesterday that I will have to get up at night to feed Charlie soon. You can't do it anymore because you're getting too big."

Kelly sighed, "I can still do it. I'm just tired," she yawned. "But I think it's a good idea for you to learn. We're going to have a couple of new mouths to feed soon, and I don't know how that's all going to work if I have to feed three babies at night."

"Oh, I know. Aunt Sally explained it all to me. She said she's going to stay with us for a while once the twins are born and help out."

"Oh, she did, did she?" Kelly smiled. She still didn't know how she felt about that. Aunt Sally had suggested it several times. Boone suggested it, too. She supposed it would have to be the new reality, even though she liked her own privacy.

Right now, Kelly was emotional. It didn't help that her entire body felt like a giant pumpkin, and she cried at the drop of a hat. Her hormones were all over the place. Tears streamed down her face as she tried to wipe away the evidence. Hopefully Lily didn't notice her losing it again. It was a daily occurrence.

"Are you crying?"

Well, that wasn't very inconspicuous. "No!" She wiped her face quickly.

"Yes, you are! I'm calling Aunt Sally. You need her, don't you?"

"I need a lot of things," Kelly said as she sniffled. She couldn't understand why the tears were falling. She felt sad for some reason. She couldn't put her finger on it, but it had something to do with Boone. He seemed like he was hiding something. Though they'd been through couples therapy again, and it went very well, something was wrong.

Maybe she just missed life before kids when they were carefree without responsibilities. Sure, she enjoyed fostering Lily and Charlie, and that was going well, too, but she missed the days when she didn't have so many responsibilities.

Or, maybe she was just tired. That's what it was. She needed a nap.

"Can you watch Charlie? No, actually, you're right," she said. "Why don't you call Aunt Sally? Ask her to come over and watch the baby so I can have a nap."

"I can watch him. I've been getting good at it.

"I don't doubt you can, but I'd feel better with Aunt Sally here to help you if something happens. Babies are full of surprises sometimes. Just when you change them and get them ready to go for a walk, explosive diarrhea shoots up their back."

Lily burst out laughing, and so did Kelly. Charlie filled his pants so many times, they both knew it was true. At least the laughter kicked her out of her pity-party mood. But she was still exhausted. She felt like she could sleep for a week.

As soon as Aunt Sally arrived, she headed straight for Kelly. "Are you okay, sweetheart? Maybe you should take some liquid vitamins. Dr. Thomas told you they're easier for you to absorb. When was the last time you took some?"

"I don't know." Kelly was sick of being a lab rat. She was sick of everyone treating her like a delicate flower. These babies need to come out now! Her body couldn't take much more. "I just need some sleep. Why don't you guys get the baby ready and take him down to the docks? He likes the sound of the ocean."

"Honey, I'm not doing anything until I tuck you in bed. I brought you some of my gluten-free chicken noodle soup. First, you're going to have some, and then to bed you go, young lady. And I don't want to hear any if-ands-or-butts about it. Do you hear me?"

"Yes, ma'am!" Kelly gobbled up her aunt's soup and the two of them walked her to bed. They tucked her in, turned off the light, and pulled down the shades. The twins did somersaults inside her belly as if to thank her for nourishing them. She sighed and yawned until her eyelids wouldn't stay open any longer.

In seconds, Kelly fell fast asleep.

Fool Or Not

The stage was set. Boone was nervous almost all the time. He hated keeping this from Kelly, especially right now. She was not herself. The twin pregnancy was hard on her body and emotions. He walked around on eggshells most days.

Their communication skills had really improved since they finished couples therapy, but it killed him to keep pretending everything was okay. It wasn't okay, it was far from it. His buddy Jimmy was due any day now, and Lily was the bait.

Boone was told they had guys watching her 24/7. If anything happened to that little girl, he'd never forgive himself. She was like a daughter to him now. Her short stature made him think she was younger than her age, but then he had to remind himself that she was actually a mother. Hard to believe. If he didn't know her, he'd think she was maybe ten.

When he texted Jimmy her picture, the guy flipped. He praised him for finding her and told her to hang on to her. "Keep her somewhere safe, bud. She's a special order. You have no idea how happy you just made some prince in the Middle East. He's paying good money for her safe return. You should make a lot of money on her."

The whole thing made Boone sick.

John told him to ask his buddy a lot of questions, and so he did. Too many, in his opinion. He sounded like he was becoming suspicious. "Why are you asking me all these questions, bud?" Jimmy drilled him. "You better not be a snitch. I don't have a problem putting a bullet through your head. You know that."

"Settle down, Jimmy!" Boone played the part. "You know

me better than that."

"How come you never told me you got married?"

How did he find that out? That meant Jimmy was digging. "I-um, I didn't think it was important. I met a tourist on a bear guide," he tried to downplay it. "We don't really get along that great." Boone cringed when he said it. It was partly true. They used to have issues because of what they had gone through, but he didn't exactly tell the truth.

He hoped God would forgive him.

Lately, he felt distant from the Lord. That was his fault. He was so busy, he barely had time to pray, let alone read the Bible. He knew he should. He also knew he would go through hills and valleys like this. He learned that lesson while he was still in prison. The pastor explained why it happens. "Discipline, it's how you know you're his," he told him.

Boone wondered if the Lord was disciplining him now. He should have told his wife what was happening with Lily long ago when he first realized who she was. What if she never forgives him? What if this ends their marriage once and for all?

Okay, God, you got my attention. I'm sorry I've been so distant. I gather you want me to come clean with Kelly. If I tell her, then please protect her.

It was decided. He'd tell his wife everything. He just had to finish up with John. He wanted him to meet him at the detachment today. It was a rare day off. Really, he just wanted to spend it with his wife, but he knew they had to go over the final details before Jimmy arrived. They had intel that told them his friend was arriving with a couple of big shots who had more pull than Jimmy. They were trying to catch the big fish, so this was great. Maybe they could close this ring down for good.

Stay out of Alaska, you creeps!

"Boone! You with us?" John interrupted his thoughts. "You okay? You're not getting cold feet, are you? We need you in on this."

"I'm fine. I have a lot on my mind."

"Of course you do. That's what you signed up for. I might

remind you that this was your idea. You started this whole mess, and now you have to finish it."

Boon knew that full well. He didn't need the guy reminding him. He had put his family and the entire community at risk. Now it was time to pay the reaper. Boone looked at his watch, wondering how long they were going to rehash the plan.

"Got somewhere to be?" John drilled him again.

"No."

"Then pay attention. We don't know when exactly they'll arrive. It could be today, tomorrow, or next week. We have to stay sharp. Keep your eyes peeled. And Boone, don't rely on your buddy Jimmy letting you know he's here. We've watched these guys before. They blend in. They pretend they're tourists. Sometimes they arrive in the middle of the night. Stay sharp, everyone."

That was it. Thankfully, the meeting was over, and he could head home soon. It was all he could do to keep his eyes open. Sure, they'd planned this for weeks, but Boone dreaded going over and over the plan. Not only did it turn his stomach, but it gave him a bellyache. He'd already been to the bathroom all morning, and now again, this afternoon. Man, would he be glad when it was over.

"Hey, Boone, can I have a word with you privately?" the police chief asked him as the rest of the force started leaving the meeting. He nodded and met John in a quiet corner. He wondered what this was about.

"So, I just wanted to say I'm here for you...as a friend. I may be your boss in front of the guys, but I know you and Kelly personally, and I just wanted to say hang in there. This kind of stuff isn't for everyone. I can understand completely if you call it quits with the force after this. You've been through a lot."

Why would he even think that?

"No, I enjoy peacekeeping. Really, I do. This situation is just nerve-wracking."

"That's an understatement. You haven't told Kelly anything yet, have you?"

"No, but I think…"

"Boone, don't be a fool! The less she knows, the better."

Sighing, Boone rubbed his red beard. It didn't seem to matter what he thought; his hands were tied. How was he supposed to move forward if he couldn't tell his wife what was bothering him, or what was about to go down?

The man shook his hand and patted him on the back. He reassured him that everything was going to work out, but Boone wasn't so sure. What if it backfired? What if his wife never forgives him? If you ask him, the more she knows, the better. He knew Kelly, and she liked to be prepared.

He needed to prepare her.

It was decided. Despite what John wanted him to do, he was going to tell Kelly anyway. She needed to know for her own safety. He was determined to tell her as soon as possible. He would tell her everything tonight.

Fool or not.

No Safe Place

I t took a long time to get the baby ready for his walk. Lily was thankful that Kelly insisted that Aunt Sally help her. It was hard being a mother. Lily wondered if she was doing it right. The diapers were hard to put on a squiggly baby.

Kelly was right. Just when they were ready to go, Charlie pooped up his back, all over the little blue sleeper she spent a long time snapping up. It was worse than a little doll. Dolls don't puke and poop, or need to be fed all the time. They just lay there without moving or making a sound.

Sometimes, Lily wished Charlie were a doll.

But he wasn't. He looked too much like the older brother. She could see the resemblance now. The baby had his features. He was probably Charlie's dad. She couldn't get him to leave her alone, even though the guy on the phone told him not to touch her. *He didn't listen.*

Lily squeezed her eyes shut and tried to forget. It was such a painful time. It seemed like another lifetime ago. All those nights she cried in her room. It was the past. She had to leave it there. She had to move on.

Kelly and Boone were nice, much nicer than the group home. She was glad she pushed so hard for Kelly to take her home. She felt a little guilty about that, but it all worked out in the end.

They were just like parents to her. They put her mother to shame. She wasn't even going to think about her stepfather. As far as she was concerned, he didn't exist. He never cared for her anyway. She sure didn't miss that idiot.

But still...not a word from her mother. She thought

maybe she'd call sometime, but the social worker told her not to expect it. Still, Lily hoped. She just wanted her to see her cute little Charlie. Maybe then she would love her.

It didn't matter. She had a new mom now and a new aunt. Aunty Sally was more like a grandmother to her, and she taught her everything. She scooped the baby up in a second when he pooped all over, got him changed and ready all over again, and they were finally out the door.

It was a beautiful fall day outside. The sun was warm and bright, and Lily inhaled the salty fall air. She listened to the seagulls crying overhead, and squinted toward the dock, deciding that's where she would take Charlie today.

After all, he did like the sound of the ocean.

"So, my dear," Aunt Sally broke the silence. "What do you want to do with the rest of your life? Maybe you want to go to school?"

Leave it to Aunt Sally to keep asking her that. The lady didn't know how to give up. Lily could tell she meant well, but she really didn't want to talk about that. School was not for her. She was a dumbo.

"I'm a mom now," Lily smiled.

"I know you are, young lady," Aunt Sally smiled back, "but that doesn't mean you can't learn other things. You have the rest of your life still. You can become anything."

"So, being a mom isn't enough?"

"It's enough. I think you know what I mean. You're a bright girl."

"No, I'm not."

"Yes, you are! If you weren't, you never would have made it this far. Lily, you've been through more in your short life than most people do in a lifetime. That's huge. Other people could learn from you. You could help people. You could be a social worker, a teacher, or a nurse. Like I said, you could be anything."

Lily didn't know what to say to that. Nobody had ever called her bright before. Nobody had ever told her she could help people. Her stepfather told her she was good for nothing. Her own mother called her a retard.

"I'll think about it, Aunt Sally."

"Okay, but just remember. You have people in your life who love you. God loves you, too. He wants the best for you."

Not this again. They all kept pushing God at her. He hadn't helped her so far, so she didn't expect anything now. Kelly drilled her for hours and hours. Now, Aunt Sally.

"Stop with the God talk, already!"

"Oh, okay. I didn't mean to annoy you."

Now Lily felt bad. The lady was just trying to be nice. Lily wished she could control her mouth better. It had improved since Kelly took her off gluten, but she still felt like she had a mouth full of marbles. She wished she could at least control her temper.

"I'm sorry, Aunt Sally," Lily bit her lip. She wanted to try to be a better person. Maybe if she tried hard enough, she wouldn't make all these mistakes.

"It's okay, my dear," Aunt Sally told her. "You are entitled to your own opinion. It's okay to speak your mind. Just remember, the tone of your voice sets the mood and determines how people respond to you."

Aunt Sally was right. She did sound snarky.

"You're so smart."

"You are too, my girl. You just don't know it yet. You have so much potential. I love you so much!" Aunt Sally put her arm around her and squeezed as they stood at the end of the street looking at the dock in front of them.

It was filled with boats of all kinds. Sailboats. Fishing boats. It's where Boone docked his boat. She could see it in the corner of the bay where he always parked it. In her opinion, it was the best schooner around. She loved riding on it when she first came to stay with them. It got her over her fear of boats pretty quickly.

Lily wasn't really afraid of boats like she told Kelly, just one boat: The boat she escaped from. It was an ugly lime green, just like the boat docked to the left of them. Wait, it had a big lady on the side, just like the one she was looking at right now.

Panic struck her hard. She started to hyperventilate.

"What's the matter, my dear?"

Lily couldn't speak. Her heavy breathing consumed her. Sweat poured down her forehead and nose. "I-I don't feel well."

Aunt Sally guided her to the nearest bench while she pushed the stroller. "Sit. Breathe. Put your head between your legs. It's okay. YOU'RE OKAY!"

Lily knew it was NOT okay. When she finally slowed her breath down, her head started pounding. She inhaled and let the warm sun wash over her face. She tilted her head up to the sky, but the clouds started spinning. They spun around and around like a merry-go-round until she finally threw up her lunch on the ground.

"I need to go home," she cried.

"Tell me what's happening."

"NO!"

Nobody understood. Nobody could help her. *Not even God.* There was nowhere she could hide. It didn't matter how good she had it. It didn't matter how safe she felt.

They found her anyway.

Just Survive

Kelly woke to the sound of smoke alarms going off. What was happening? She was half asleep still, as she rolled out of bed and rubbed her eyes. The bedroom door was closed, but smoke was starting to seep through the space underneath.

She grabbed her robe lying on the edge of the bed and quickly wrapped it around her oversized belly. This was not happening.

"Boone? Lily? Help!"

Nobody answered. She was stuck there. She couldn't open the door, or she'd let more smoke into the bedroom. It was already getting hard to breathe. She ran to the window, but their bedroom was on the second story. She definitely couldn't jump.

I can open the window.

Kelly pulled as hard as she could, but it was stuck. It was an old two-story with windows that didn't open easily. Boone usually opened them with his strong arms.

"HELP!"

She ran to the half-bath in the bedroom and wet a facecloth. Then she held it over her nose and mouth and searched for her cell phone. Where was it? She looked at the nightstand. She looked at the dresser. Nothing.

The glass. She could break the glass.

Kelly looked around for something she could use to break the window. She grabbed a candle and was about to break the glass when she heard someone stomping around downstairs. "HELP! I'M UP HERE!"

She dropped the candle and went for the door instead.

Kelly started banging on the door, afraid to open it. "HERE! I'M IN HERE!" Someone must have seen the smoke and called the fire department. At least they were here already.

Lord, ME!

BANG, BANG, BANG!

"I'M UP HERE!"

Kelly could hear heavy boots coming up the stairs toward her. What a relief. They were getting her out. *They were getting her out!*

Suddenly, the door flung open to two men wearing black ski masks. These were not firemen. Kelly didn't know who they were.

They grabbed her arms and escorted her down the smoky stairwell. "Come on!" One of them said, before the whole place burns down. "Get her to the truck out back. Hurry up!"

Kelly coughed and gagged through the smoke, and they rushed her through the kitchen. The curtains were on fire. Things were knocked over. She could barely see. Smoke was everywhere. "WAIT! WHAT'S GOING ON?"

"Keep your mouth shut, and MOVE!"

When they got to the back door, someone spun her around and blindfolded her. They were hurting her arms, and she could feel them dragging her outside. They lifted her body into a truck and slammed the door.

What was going on?

Lord Jesus, I need you NOW! PLEASE HELP ME!

The truck sped off fast, and her body bounced around, hitting the side of the truck. "Put her seatbelt on!" She heard a voice tell someone else. Then, the man sitting beside her reached over her, squishing her stomach. He pulled the seatbelt across her pregnant belly. Kelly noticed his smelly underarms. It repulsed her.

"WHERE ARE YOU TAKING ME?"

"Shut up, you stupid broad!"

The guy beside her elbowed her in the side. It hurt so bad, she cried in pain. "Please don't do that! I'M PREGNANT!"

"No kidding!"

Her body bounced around as they sped off-road somewhere out of town. Kelly felt dizzy and nauseous like she was about to throw up. Her side still ached, and she clutched her belly to protect it.

She cried softly, hoping they didn't hear. The truck was so loud like there wasn't even a muffler. But they heard her anyway.

"SHUT UP! Or, I'll elbow you again!

Tears streamed down Kelly's cheeks. She sucked in the pain and tried to be quiet. Instead, she prayed silently. *Yea, though I walk through the valley of the shadow of death, I will fear no evil; thy rod and thy staff they comfort me.*

Memories of when Boone taught her that verse the first time flooded back in. He was there then, and He's here now. She could feel Him. He was her peace in the storm. And right now, she needed to be calm, not just for herself, but for her babies.

She would give them no reason to harm them. *None!*

"It's just around the bend," the guy in the passenger seat said. "Beyond those bushes. You see it?"

"Yah, I see it. You sure nobody knows about it?"

"Nobody."

All Kelly could do was listen now. She figured they were on the road for about twenty minutes, maybe half an hour. She knew pretty well all the roads leading in and out of Angoon. Boone had taken her on an ATV to explore the area several times. She tried to picture whereabouts they were, but she wasn't sure.

The truck came to a stop, and Kelly could hear the driver turn off the engine. They just sat there and waited for something. Nobody said a word.

Kelly just listened. She could hear ravens croaking. The smell of fall was in the air, mixed with a campfire. The inviting aroma filled her nostrils. Maybe they were hunters. But what did they want with her?

"Okay, get her out," the passenger ordered. He sounded familiar, but she couldn't put her finger on where she had heard him before. It sounded like the man was deliberately lowering his voice so she couldn't recognize him.

Just listen, she told herself. Don't care, just survive.

A door opened, and she felt two men lowering her out of the truck. They walked her arm in arm through dry leaves, struggling with her as she lost her footing. "Come on, lady," one of them complained. "Pick up the pace. We ain't got all day."

Kelly didn't respond. *Don't care, just survive.*

They took her into a musty-smelling cabin and shut the door. "Sit down!" They ordered her. Someone shoved her down and made her sit on a kitchen chair. By the feel of it, it was an old wooden one.

"Use the duct tape and tie her up."

She could hear the sound of duct tape unravelling. Then someone pulled her hands behind the chair and taped them also.

"Do her feet too."

Someone bent down and wrapped duct tape around and around her ankles. They taped her legs to the chair, too. She could feel it cold against her bare legs, wishing she had worn her pyjamas instead of her nightgown.

Her bare feet hurt from walking through the damp prickles outside. She was sure she had some slivers in her toes, but that was the least of her worries.

"Now what?" one of them said.

"We wait. Just like he wanted. They'll bring the other one soon."

The other one? Kelly wondered what that meant. Who were they bringing? Could it be Boone? Had he gotten himself into trouble? Was that why he was acting so weird lately? He thought she didn't notice, but it was written all over his face.

Something was wrong.

Did he owe money or something? All sorts of scenarios played out in her mind. She gave her head a shake to try and snap out of it. She had to trust the Lord. He got her through so much; how would he not protect her now?

"Stop that, lady. Stop moving your head like that."

Kelly didn't respond. He must have seen her shake her

head. What did he care if she did that? These guys were ignorant. They didn't have much patience with her. She tried to keep her head as still as possible.

The guy came right up to her. She stood there for a moment and kicked her bare feet with his boot. "Do it again, you stupid broad. I dare you."

Kelly kept her head perfectly still, but it wasn't good enough. The man suddenly slapped the side of her face hard. It stung so bad she wanted to cry, but she didn't. She wouldn't give him the satisfaction.

Don't care, she told herself. Just survive.

Alive

B y the time Boone arrived, his house was fully engulfed in flames. He stood there watching the horror unfold: Windows shattered, hoses sprayed, and black smoke billowed. Why didn't he leave the police station earlier? Did it really matter that he stayed an extra hour after everyone left, just to go over the plan again? John suggested he needed another run through, but he didn't have to listen to the man. He could have been home already. He could have prevented this. *What was he trying to prove?*

Boone beat himself up as he rushed over to Barry, the fire chief. "Where's my wife? Where's Lily and the baby?"

He headed for the burning front door.

"Hold your horses," Barry shouted, "Where do you think you're going? Are you nuts? You can't go inside."

"MY WIFE! DID SHE GET OUT?"

"Buddy, I-I don't know! All I can tell you is the house was gone before we even got here. It wasn't structurally sound. I couldn't send my guys in. I'm sorry!"

"YOU'RE SORRY?"

Boone pushed forward, trying to get into the house, but two firefighters held him back. They wouldn't let him enter the house. He struggled and fought against them, trying to break free. They pulled him backward to the street in front. "STOP! BOONE, JUST STOP! We won't know anything until we put the fire out.

"THAT'S TOO LATE!

Boone dropped to his knees and sobbed. "My wife! *Oh God, please don't let her be in there! PLEASE!*"

A first responder ran up to him and asked him if he was okay. He didn't answer. He held his head and screamed, "DID ANYONE SEE KELLY?"

Boone got up and darted around from person to person. "Did you see my wife? Do you know if she left the house? Did any one of you see Kelly?" AND WHERE'S JOHN? He should be here somewhere. Maybe he knows? JOHN?"

The entire neighbourhood watched him lose it. The firefighters and first responders looked dumbfounded. The two guys who led him away from his house stood their ground and wouldn't let him anywhere near the property.

"KELLY!" He shouted.

If this was it, then he was done too. There is no coming back from this one. How did it start? He was meticulous with the wiring. It was upgraded, and so was the furnace. How could this even happen? "WHY, LORD? WHY?"

Boone felt a gentle hand on his shoulder then. "My boy, it's gonna be okay." It was Aunty Sally. She stood beside him with her arm around his shoulder. She pulled him in and gave him a long hug. "Kelly! Is she in there, aunty?"

The woman sighed. He knew what that meant.

Then he heard a baby cry. It was Charlie in the stroller. He wiped his eyes. "You were out for a walk? Where is she? Where are Kelly and Lily? They were with you then?"

"No, my boy. Just Lily and the baby."

"I don't understand." He shook his head. He didn't want to piece the puzzle together. Not now. Not if there is still hope. He needed to ask Lily. Surely Kelly was with Lily. She was always with Lily. "Lily? Where are you?"

Boone spun around looking for the girl, but she wasn't there. "Where's Lily?"

"I left her at the dock. She wasn't feeling well. She needed some air, and the baby started crying, so I headed home. That's when I found the house on fire. I'm sorry, Boone. We left her asleep upstairs."

"NO! NO! NO!"

This was not happening. He'd go down to the dock and talk to Lily. This wasn't true. Surely Kelly had gone with them. Aunt Sally was wrong. She always goes for a walk with Lily and the baby. Probably, Aunt Sally didn't know she headed down there after them.

"I-I have to go find her. I'm sure she's with Lily. She wouldn't leave them."

"Boone, STOP!" Aunt Sally said abruptly as she moved the stroller back and forth, soothing the crying baby. "You need to prepare yourself for the worst. She was sleeping upstairs. Lily and I tucked her in a few hours ago. She was exhausted."

"WHY? WHY DID YOU LEAVE HER?"

Boone was out of control. He would NOT accept this. Maybe she woke up. Maybe she followed them. She could have gone for a walk. She could have left the house. She could be anywhere. Not up there. Not...in that burning house.

"Boone, we need you to come with us," a first responder told him. "We can take you to the clinic and hope for the best. Maybe she's there."

"Yes, Boone. Let these men do their jobs and go with Laura. She knows what she's doing. She can take you to the clinic and get things sorted. If Kelly left the house, she knew to go there in an emergency. It's the next best thing to a hospital. It's worth a shot."

Boone knew what they were doing, but he was too tired and distraught to fight them. They wanted him to leave. They wanted him to calm down. They'd sedate him if they could. He knew the drill.

"Fine," he sighed. "Let's go check the clinic. He headed for the passenger seat.

"We need you to ride in the back."

Boone looked around at all the people staring. He looked back at the burning house. It was a scene out of an apocalyptic movie. If he couldn't do anything here, he'd turn the entire town upside down. Why not start at the clinic?

"Fine. I'll get in the *back* of the ambulance."

As soon as he climbed into the vehicle, two other first responders laid him down on the gurney. They wrapped him with a silver blanket and assessed him. "He's in shock. Just keep him warm." They took his vitals and talked to him, but he didn't have a clue what they were saying. Frankly, he didn't care.

Boone was numb. His body started trembling even though he tried to calm down. He took a breath and allowed them to put an oxygen mask on his face. He inhaled deeply and listened to his Aunt Sally's even-tempered voice outside.

"Thank you for taking the baby," she said to someone. "I need to go back to the dock to get Lily. I can't leave her there alone. Not now."

"No problem," the voice answered his aunt. "We'll take good care of this little guy."

Then someone closed the ambulance doors, and the vehicle slowly drove away from the horrific scene. Boone fought back tears as he lay there with the first responders fussing over him. "You're okay, Boone. Just try to breathe."

How could he breathe when Kelly was missing?

Please find her Jesus! ALIVE!

The Getaway

Lily was glad Aunt Sally took Charlie back home. She needed to think. She was tired of running, but maybe there was no choice. Maybe she had to leave Charlie somewhere safe: With the McKenzies. Boone and Kelly would protect him. She knew he was in good hands with them.

She took a deep breath of warm, salty air, mixed with a hint of campfire smoke. It was perfect while it lasted. She knew when it was time to go. It was now or never. She'd have to make her escape quickly, before anyone noticed.

If she didn't, they'd all be in danger.

There was no way the brothers were going to abduct her again. She had to get away before they came looking. The seagulls screamed above, telling her to move quickly, so that's what she did. There were numerous boats in the harbour to choose from, but she knew Boone's schooner the best. More importantly, she knew where he kept the spare key.

Boone would never forgive her for taking it, but it was better than the alternative. She could live with Boone's wrath. He had been nothing but kind to her. But what she couldn't live with was what they might do to her if they found her.

Or, do to them for fostering her.

Lily walked down to the water, scurrying past all kinds of fishing vessels going about their day. Tourists were standing there with fishing rods, boarding a few different boats. It was a popular place. She hoped she would blend right in.

She ignored the lime green boat with the lady on the side and made a beeline to Boone's boat. She looked around to make sure nobody saw her and reached under the dock where the spare key was hidden.

Good, it's still there.

Surely, it wouldn't be that hard to drive the boat. She hadn't actually done it before, but how hard could it be? She'd seen Boone do it several times.

Lily climbed on board and bent down to hide when she heard a voice. Startled, she turned around to see the uniform. *Great! Just what she needed. The police.*

"You're not trying to steal Boone's boat, are you, Lily?"

Alarm washed over her face. She was caught red-handed. It was the police chief. "Hi John," she smiled. "I was just... pretending."

"Sure, you were. How about you come down from there and let me take you home? Do Boone and Kelly know where you are?"

"No."

"I thought so. Why don't you get out of there and let me take you home? I'm sure they're worried about you. Besides, you don't want me telling Boone about this little adventure, do you?"

"No."

The man looked sincere. He was a friend of her foster parents, and that meant he could be trusted. Maybe she just over-reacted. Maybe the lime green boat wasn't even the brothers' boat. It was probably her emotions again. Kelly told her they would go up and down for the next few months. That was the truth.

"Why don't you come sit in the car? I'll make sure you get home safe and sound, and nobody will be the wiser. Just our little secret," he winked.

Lily smiled and followed the man to his car.

She had let her emotions get the best of her. Why would she want to leave the best people she'd ever met, anyway? Kelly was like a sister-mom to her. Nobody ever treated her like that before. She and Boone actually cared.

"Should I sit in the front with you?" She asked.

"Well now, how would that look to everyone else?" he

told her. "You should probably sit in the back." He looked around nervously, like he was worried someone would see.

"But I'm not under arrest, am I?"

"Well, you were trying to steal Boone's boat, weren't you?"

Tears filled Lily's bright blue eyes. She hoped the man was kidding, but there was something about him that alarmed her. Maybe he really was going to arrest her after all.

"I guess I was trying to steal it," she answered him.

"You guess? Well, now, Lily, either you were or you weren't. Which one is it?"

"You said you would forget about it."

"Why, yes, I did. But criminals still sit in the back. Now GET IN!" He scolded her like he meant to arrest her. Maybe she'd better listen. She didn't want to go to jail.

He looked around nervously again and slammed the door behind her a little too hastily. She sulked in the back seat, locked in there like a prisoner.

"You're taking me home, right?"

The man didn't respond. He got on the radio and said something in code. Lily had no idea what it meant. She just kept her mouth shut. They drove the backroads around town and then headed on a side road.

This was not the way home.

She wondered if she should say anything or if he would get mad again. Finally, as they continued driving into the thick forest, panic set in. Where was he taking her? What was happening? Maybe she'd better say something now.

"Where are we going?"

"Oh, honey, why would I tell you that?" He laughed. He got on the radio again and reported something. It sounded like he told the other guy that they were ten minutes out and he was arriving with the prize.

Was she the prize?

Lily started to breathe heavily. She could feel a panic attack coming on. Kelly explained what that was. It kept happening to her. Sweat beaded down her forehead as she started hyperventilating and whimpering.

"Shut up, kid!"

She screamed and kicked the back of his seat, trying to get out of the door. They were locked. She was caged in like an animal with no way to get out.

"Keep it up, Sunshine, and it will be the last thing you do."

Lily immediately sucked in her tears and stopped. She knew he was serious. Was she going to die today? What was he going to do to her? She looked around as they rolled into a long driveway amongst some tall spruce trees. Hidden behind them was an old cabin with smoke coming out of the chimney.

She said nothing as they came to a stop.

John left her in the vehicle and headed into the cabin. Lily realized this was her chance to escape. She kicked the doors and shook the cage that separated the front from the back of the police car. It was solid. There was no breaking out of that.

Lily started to bawl.

A few minutes later, a guy came out of the cabin with John. He was also a cop. She recognized him. He was a young rookie from town. His name was Danny. Then two others came out. Her heart sank when she saw them.

THE BROTHERS!

I Told You

Boone was given something to calm him down while he rested at the clinic. It was either that, or he would have to go to the hospital in Juneau. Angoon didn't have a hospital, but it was times like this that he wished they did. Leaving now was not an option. Not when Kelly was still missing.

He'd been resting since they brought him in there, but his blood pressure was still high, which prompted them to want to fly him to the hospital. But no way. One more hour was all he'd give them, and then he'd get the heck out of there.

"It's still high, Mr. McKenzie," the nurse said. "Your blood pressure has come down a little bit, but we'd like to see it drop much lower than that. Are you sure you're feeling okay? 200 over 124 is not good."

"Yes! Now get me out of here!"

"Dr. Thomas is going to video conference with you in about half an hour. He'll make the final decision. He wants to make sure you're okay. Besides, the fire chief is coming to speak with you. I guess they have some answers for you."

Finally, Boone had been lying there for hours with no answers. He looked at his watch, and still no word from John. What a time to be M.I.A. Did he go on vacation or something? It didn't make sense.

And where was Aunt Sally? She and Lily should have been back hours ago. They would have come to see him, not left him lying there alone. It was the worst place to be at the worst time. He just wanted out of there so he could find his wife.

She wasn't in the house. He wasn't accepting that.

Boone decided to close his eyes and rest his brain for a while longer. There was nothing else he could do but wait. He prayed under his breath as he blocked out everything except God's word. He knew that's what he needed. He loved the Psalms. They always comforted him. He ran them through his mind until he remembered one.

"God is our refuge and strength, an ever-present help in trouble."

That was an understatement. Boone had recited Psalm 46:1 so many times in the last few years that he could say it backwards. Through every miscarriage. Through all their disagreements and communication problems. So many memories rose to the surface.

God always showed up through the pain. *Always!* Boone could honestly say God had never let him down. *Not once.* Not in prison, not during the incident with the Kushtaka in the bush, not with the miscarriages. *Never.*

You're so good, God!

If Kelly were dead, he'd know it. He was sure she was still alive. He could feel it. She was out there somewhere, and something strange was going on. *I gotta get out of here!*

Boone realized another hour had already gone by. He wasn't waiting anymore. He unhooked his IV and sat up on the bed. Where were his clothes? He had to get dressed. Enough was enough. There was nothing wrong with him.

"Mr. McKenzie! What are you doing?" A nurse ran over to him. "We have your doctor on a video call. Please wait. He wants to talk to you."

"Oh...Fine!" Boone complained. It better not take too long. He had to get out of there and find his wife. This was crazy.

A nurse brought a computer tablet to him, and it was Dr. Thomas on the screen. "Boone, I want you to take it easy. Let the authorities handle it. I know you, and I know it's hard for you to let them, but they will do the investigating. My main concern is YOU right now. I want you to take care of yourself. Your blood pressure is a concern, and I'd like the nurse to take another reading right now. Nurse? Are you there?"

The nurse confirmed and put the blood pressure cuff on his arm again. It automatically filled with air and took another reading. "150 over 86. It's gone down quite a bit. What do you think, Doctor?"

Boone knew he was fine. They were just fussing over him for nothing.

"I'd still like to see it lower, but Boone, I want you to promise me you'll go to your aunts and rest. No heroics."

"Fine! Just get me out of here."

"Nurse, you can discharge him. And Boone, we're all praying for Kelly. I understand she is missing now. Or, at least that's what the report I got from the fire chief says."

"I hadn't heard from the fire chief yet."

Boone was thankful to hear this. He knew Kelly wasn't in the house. Where was the fire chief? Barry was supposed to fill him in on the findings.

"And one more thing, Boone. I've let the authorities know that Kelly is in a very vulnerable state. She's heading into her 35th week of pregnancy. If she's stressed, the twins will be stressed as well. I've ordered my medical staff to fly to Angoon tomorrow morning. They will be at the clinic on standby. If she's escaped the fire, as we're led to believe, she could be disoriented and have smoke inhalation. The authorities are out looking for her, so let them do their job. Just go home. I mean…to your aunt's place. I'm so sorry, Boone!"

As soon as the video call ended, Boone went for his pile of clothes and got himself dressed. He headed out of the room and down the hall. Barry was waiting to brief him on the findings. *Finally, some answers!*

"So, what did you find?"

"She wasn't in the house!"

"I TOLD YOU!"

And Boone, you're not gonna like this, but there were signs of forced entry. We think someone abducted her. A neighbour saw her drive away with some men in a black truck.

"WHAT?"

"And...we found accelerant."

"What do you mean, you found accelerant? You mean someone deliberately set the fire and kidnapped my wife at the same time?"

"That's what it looks like."

Boone's anger consumed him. He stormed past Barry and out the double doors of the clinic. Whoever did this was going to pay. It didn't take a brain surgeon to figure out what was going on. This was Jimmy's doing!

They were on to him.

Sorry

By the time Boone got to his Aunt Sally's place, it was already dark. There were no lights on. No signs of life. Where was she? Could she be at a friend's house? Maybe she and Lily were with the baby there. He figured it was her neighbour, Verna, a couple of doors down, whom she asked to watch Charlie. He'd go there next.

The night air gave him a chill as he stood there to catch his breath. The whole thing turned his stomach. He tried to calm down like the doctor told him to, but it wasn't going to be easy. Something was seriously wrong.

Boone grabbed his cell phone and tried to call his aunt again. Just like before, she wasn't answering. It went straight to voicemail. What on earth was going on? He walked along the crunchy gravel road until he got to Verna's. Thank the Lord, a light was on. He knocked at the door.

Footsteps to the door greeted him. "Boone! I'm so sorry!"

"Sorry? What do you mean?"

"Your house! The fire!"

Boone thought something worse for a moment, then brushed it off. He couldn't care less about that old house. He'd gotten it for a song anyway. Material things could be replaced, but his family could not. "Oh, yeah, the house."

"Are you okay?"

"I will be, as soon as I find my family. Do you know where they are?"

"No, we were watching Charlie all afternoon, but a deputy came and got the baby. I guess your aunt is at the police station, and they were taking him to her."

"Why is she at the police station?"

"I don't know."

Boone rushed away immediately. "Thank you, Verna." He raised an arm as he headed to the police station. It was quite a walk. He should have taken Aunt Sally's old Honda, but he didn't know where she kept the keys.

The night air nipped at him now that the sun had set. It was already November, so what did he expect? Under normal circumstances, this time of year would be much cooler. It was like they were having a second summer.

He passed by several houses with their lights on. He could see them gathered at the kitchen table. Smells of different kinds of meals wafted into the air as he went by. It was inviting, but he knew his stomach could wait.

Boone finally arrived at the police station. "JOHN! I've been trying to call you all day! WHAT ON EARTH IS GOING ON?"

"Just settle down. We have the whole force out looking for Kelly!"

"Where's my aunt?

"You just missed her. I sent her home with one of my officers. She was exhausted."

Boone was missing some pieces. None of this made sense. Why was Aunt Sally so exhausted? Why wouldn't she just take the baby home where she could rest? Why go to the police station to begin with?

And more importantly, why couldn't he get a hold of anyone?

"I tried to phone her, and it went straight to voicemail. So did yours. Doesn't anyone know how to communicate around here? It's not that hard to pick up a phone!"

John screwed up his face. He seemed annoyed that he was upset. You'd think the man would have a heart for his situation. Not only did someone deliberately set his house on fire, but they also abducted his wife. That alone would be cause for compassion. But not John, he was as hard-nosed as he always was.

"Sit down, Boone! There's a lot you don't know."

Boone slowly took a seat next to the police chief's desk. Whatever he had to say better be good, because he had to go look for his wife. He wasn't going to leave it up to the Angoon police department. They were rusty and poorly trained. Boone wanted to say that for a long time, but he held his tongue. *Lord! Set a guard over my mouth.*

"I'm listening."

"Now, when you were off taking a snooze at the clinic, we found out a few things."

Boone wanted to tell the man off. What right did he have to pick on him? It's not like he had a choice. They took him to the clinic almost against his will. He would've much rather been out looking for Kelly.

"Your aunt went to the docks to find Lily. She wasn't there. Some guy saw her get into a police car. Boone, I think Danny is in on it. And to think I trusted the punk. I should have known not to include him in the investigation. This whole thing. Our plan. It's blown right out of the water, Boone."

"YAH THINK?"

Boone shook his head. "And it's MY wife's life on the line, AND my stepdaughter's. MAN, JOHN!" He fumed, raking his hands through his hair. "We have to find them."

"And Charlie, I'm afraid."

"WHAT? NO! My aunt has him, doesn't she?"

"Well, that's the other part. I guess Danny picked up the baby from Verna and told her he was going to take him to Sally. That never happened. We think he abducted the child as well. I'm sorry."

"YOU'RE SORRY?"

"Settle down!"

"Don't tell me to settle down, John! Seriously!" Boone was so angry he wanted to scream. So, someone abducted his wife, Lily, AND the baby?" Boone knew Jimmy had to be around here somewhere.

"Don't get mad at me, it's YOUR fault. If it hadn't been for you taking things into your own hands, none of this would have happened."

"Oh, none of it? What about you? It wasn't my incompetence that got them kidnapped. You told me the guys were watching Lily at all times. What happened to that?"

Boone's anger got the best of him. He stormed off and headed for the door.

"You go through that door, and I can't protect you. We need to get you into a witness protection program, immediately."

"You know what?" Boone turned and spat back. "I'd rather die than live without my wife, so don't bother! I'm gonna find them, with or without your help. GOT IT?"

John stood with his hands on his hips. "You do NOT speak to me like that. I am your superior. I can have you suspended for that."

"Don't bother, I QUIT!"

The Hoarder

Her home felt inviting, but it wasn't his. Aunt Sally made him feel as comfortable and welcome as she could, but there was nothing that would settle him down. He missed Kelly. He worried about her constantly. It was hard not to.

"Stop pacing, Boone!" Aunt Sally told him as she stood there in her nightgown. "You can't do anything at this hour anyway, so you might as well try to get some sleep. The police are out looking for them right now."

"That's what I'm afraid of."

Aunt Sally flew her hands up. "Suit yourself. I'm going to bed!"

Her aunt turned the lights off and stormed off to her room.

Boone sat on the couch in the dark, looking at the pile of blankets his aunt had set out for him. Her home was a modest one-bedroom with no room to walk. She was what he called a hoarder. What she couldn't fit in her gift shop, she stored at home. It was wall-to-wall trinkets. Did she need to have so many?

Yawning, Boone decided to lie down. He wasn't going to sleep, only think. He kicked a pillow off the couch, which knocked one of her trinkets off the coffee table. "Sorry!" He called out. She probably didn't even hear.

Lord, I know you're with her. Please keep my Kelly safe. Please keep Lily and the baby safe, too. I don't know how to live without her. She's the best part of this old bum. Don't let anything happen to her or the twins. PLEASE!

Boone let his mind drift off into the early morning dawn. He fell in and out of sleep the whole night, restless and frustrated. He didn't even bother to change out of his clothes. He didn't even have a spare set. Everything had burned, even the nursery.

They poured out their hearts and souls into the twins' nursery. It was finally finished and ready for them to be born in a few weeks. It was a dream come true. Yet, for them, things like this always felt just out of reach.

Boone knew it was too good to be true.

But then, he knew God didn't work like that. He never wanted His children to suffer. This was something else. Someone else. This was Jimmy's doing. He knew the devil had a hold of him, and that's who he blamed.

He'd leave a note for his aunt, telling her he'd gone looking for them. He couldn't stand lying around any longer. The sun was peeking over the horizon, and he had to sneak out of town before anyone saw him. It was time to go undercover. Deep undercover.

Thankfully, Boone had trained for something like this his entire life. He knew the bush, and he knew how to hide in it. That was his plan. He'd skirt the parameter, just like he was tracking a bear. He knew how to go into stealth mode.

The only problem was that he didn't have his gear. It had burned up as well. He knew Aunt Sally had some of Uncle Doug's things in the garage still. She wouldn't like him snooping through it, but he was an avid hunter and trapper, and just about his size when he passed away from lung cancer. He loved his chewing tobacco a little too much.

Uncle Doug passed away fifteen years ago, and Aunty Sally didn't have the heart to get rid of his things. As a true hoarder does, they hold on to memories. That's why they hoard. He didn't know if he had room enough to stand in the garage, or find anything for that matter. She had wall-to-wall boxes in there that hadn't been opened in years.

Boone grabbed a banana from the table and stuffed it in

his pocket, then he found the key and headed outside. Once he opened the garage door, the musty smell wafted into his nose immediately. It looked and smelled like a rat's nest. He wasn't finding anything in this mess. *What on earth?* It was time she got rid of all this. Usually, people had kids to pass it down to, but they weren't blessed with any, just a pompous nephew who didn't want it.

Boone regretted not taking some of his uncle's things off her hands, but he didn't have the room either.

He moved some boxes aside so he could at least get in the door. Then a pile came crashing down, nearly waking the neighbourhood. He'd have to be quiet or someone would hear. He had no idea if Jimmy was waiting around the corner.

It was time to move.

Then, suddenly, an old voice shouted, "BOONE! If you wanted to borrow his things, all you had to do was ask. You didn't have to wake the neighbourhood."

It was Aunt Sally, she had snuck up on him. "You scared the living daylights out of me, Aunt Sally. I nearly had a heart attack."

"Well, it serves you right. Just ask me next time. The stuff you want is in that corner," she pointed. "See, my boy. I know you better than you think I do. He's got a bow over there. He's got all the hunting gear you'll ever need in the middle there. See the H on the boxes? I'm not that disorganized. I have a system, you know."

Boone kissed his aunt on the cheek and smiled. "I love you, Aunt Sally. You're the best!"

"Just don't get yourself killed. I need you!"

"I know.

They pressed their foreheads together and sighed.

"I've known for a long time that the police in this town were nincompoops. I don't blame you for quitting. I thought that with you on the force, they would improve. But I worried about Kelly and Lily and Charlie all night long, too. You're my only hope. Well...next to God, that is. He will guide you and protect you. Now, go find them!"

"That's the plan."

"I know your Uncle Doug would be proud of you right now."

The woman was in tears. This was all too much for her. He didn't realize how all this impacted her. He wasn't the only one it affected. She was struggling more than she let on. He was half her age. He couldn't imagine how this kind of stress affected her health. If it caused high blood pressure for him, what was it doing to her?

"Aunt Sally, I want you to do something for me. I want you to go over to the church. Stay in the dorm until I call you."

"But I lost my cell phone."

"That's what happened. Well, never mind. I'll come get you when it's safe to return home."

"But I don't want to. I want to stay here."

"You can't. I'll explain later. Just listen. Take some food and a suitcase and hibernate in there. Lock the door and don't come out for anyone. Pastor Phil will understand. He's away visiting his daughter in Seattle for a couple of months anyway. The key is under the flowerpot beside the front porch. Now hurry!"

"Why? Tell me what's going on first."

"Do you remember, Jimmy? Well, he's back. This is his doing, I'm sure of it. It's got his M.O. written all over it. Trust me on this one. I don't have time to tell you everything, just that you're not safe here."

"Okay."

"Go now!"

The woman hurried into her home, nightgown flapping in the wind. Boone turned and continued to rummage through his uncle's old things. This was going to work.

IT HAD TO!

Gob Hole

Kelly recognized the voice. It was Lily. THEY HAD LILY! She pretended not to care until the girl was safe. They tied her up in a chair next to her. She could hear the sticky sound of duct tape as they wrapped it around and around the girl.

"There! Try escaping from that!" A middle-aged man told Lily. She heard him slap her across the face pretty hard.

"Hey, numskull!" One of them said. "If you damage the merchandise, you pay for it."

Now Kelly knew what was going on. They meant to sell her. Is that what happened to her? Is that how she ended up pregnant and alone? She escaped.

Good girl!

It broke her heart to hear them treating her like that. Kelly knew they were capable. She was playing their game all afternoon. As soon as they leave, she'll be able to talk to the girl and calm her down. She whimpered beside her.

"Shut up, Kid!"

Someone kicked her chair to scare her. From the sounds of it, there were about four guys. One of them joined shortly after she arrived. The three in the truck were the ones who abducted her, but she wondered who the fourth guy was.

The men came and went all afternoon.

Kelly knew one of the voices from when she was in the truck. He was talking without disguising his voice when they first tied her up. She figured out where she knew him from. It was Danny, she was sure of it. He wasn't there for long, but she wondered what he was doing there at all. What a fool. John trusted him, and so did Boone.

The fourth guy hadn't talked yet. She didn't know what was going on with him, but the other guys asked why he was so quiet. All she heard after that was some punching. It was a fight, but it didn't last long. She just heard someone shush the other.

"Hey dude, guess what? They got him!" Kelly heard one of them say.

"Well, well, well...Derek. You just made us a pile of money. I told you to leave her alone, but maybe it wasn't such a bad idea."

Kelly wondered what all that meant. She listened for more, but all the guys rushed outside to greet the car that had just pulled up. Good! She hoped they'd stay out there so she had a chance to talk to Lily.

As soon as she heard the cabin door slam, she spoke to the girl. "Are you okay?" she whispered to her quickly. Did they hurt you?"

"NO! But they will!"

"You know them, don't you?"

"Yes! They took me from Anchorage. They wanted to sell me to some big, rich guy. Angoon was the pickup spot. That's when I jumped ship and had Charlie in the toilet."

Kelly's heart wrenched. *That poor girl.* They must have been looking for her for a while now. *What a bunch of scum bags!*

"Listen, before they come back," Kelly continued to whisper. "Do whatever they say. Don't try to fight them. Don't show any emotion. It's the only way to survive. You gotta NOT care. Just focus on surviving."

"I tried that before. It didn't get me anywhere."

She was right. They had to escape somehow, or this wasn't going to end well. But how? She was almost nine months pregnant. It wasn't going to be easy with her big belly.

"Focus on their voices. See if you can recognize anyone."

"Why? They didn't blindfold me. I can see them all."

"You can?" Kelly found that interesting. Why didn't they blindfold Lily but not her? Who were these men? Did she know them? Were they planning to let her go, but not Lily? Why would they let anyone go if they could recognize their faces?

"Quickly! Tell me who they are in case we get separated."

"Well, you got the brothers who took me. They call them the preachers. The younger one is Derek. He never touched me. He likes me, but his big fat brother is probably Charlie's dad. He wouldn't leave me alone, if you know what I mean."

Oh, she knew what she meant, and it sickened her.

"Go on! Quickly, before they come back."

"I don't know anyone else. Just John."

"Who?"

Suddenly, they all came barging in, laughing. "Aw, he looks just like you, Derek."

"He's not mine, I told you that!"

"Whatever you say, little brother."

Then, Kelly's heart wrenched. She heard a baby cry. It was Charlie. What was going on here? What had they done?

"Charlie!" Lily cried. "Give me my baby, you jerks!"

They rushed over to her and assaulted Lily again, slapping her back and forth across the face. "You don't talk unless we say so, got it?"

Lily bawled.

Charlie bawled.

The baby wouldn't stop crying, so the men passed him back and forth to each other like a football. "I don't want him," one said. Another said the same. Over and over until the baby was so frantic, Kelly couldn't stand it anymore. She had to do something.

"I can help you," she said. "Take my blind fold off, and free my hands. I'll keep the baby quiet. Come on, you need me."

She could hear the men talking amongst themselves, and one of them told another guy he'd better leave. She heard footsteps toward the door, and then someone left. A car outside started up and drove away. She had no idea what was happening and why he had left.

The baby still wailed.

Suddenly, a knife cut off her blindfold. Her eyes were blurry as he freed her hands as well. They left her legs taped to the chair.

Someone rolled a stroller over to her. "There! Now get the kid to shut up."

Kelly's eyes started to focus again, and she could see the flailing infant. He had cried himself into a dither, and he was soaking wet. He desperately needed a diaper change. Thankfully, the stroller was fully stocked with what he needed. The only problem was that she couldn't change him while sitting on a chair with a big pregnant belly.

"Do you think you could let me sit on the couch? I can't change him in this chair. I need some space. You can keep my ankles taped if you're worried I'll take off. Trust me, I'm not going anywhere."

The thugs looked at each other, and the one she assumed was Derek, cut the tape that held her to the chair and set her free. They guided her to the couch, which wasn't far from the chairs. Her body felt much better in the comfort of the couch.

"Now, give him to me." She soothed him and rocked him and sang him a lullaby. The poor child whimpered until he gave up crying. She grabbed a diaper from the stroller and twisted her body to change him. Then she changed his little wet sleeper and held him back up to her chest. "It's okay, sweetie! It's okay."

The men looked at her, dumbfounded. *Stupid men!* she wanted to say. But she didn't dare say a word. Instead, she reached into the diaper bag for a bottle. Thankfully, she found three pre-made ones left. She took out the battery-powered, portable bottle warmer she was thankful she had invested in, and in three minutes, the bottle should be ready for Charlie.

There was a little dry formula left in the can, and a jug of water they made a practice of bringing along on their walks, thankfully. But they would need much more of everything if they wanted the baby to be content.

As soon as the warmer beeped ready, Kelly gave the bottle to the baby. Instantly, he started sucking. He gulped down the bottle like a ravenous wolf, making puffing and gulping sounds as he swallowed. He was so hungry, poor little guy.

"I'm going to need diapers and some fresh water and more formula if you don't want him to cry anymore. Danny," she said, pointing him out deliberately. "Why don't you go to town and get some supplies for the baby. If you guys want this transaction to go smoothly, and it sounds like you do, then you're going to have to provide for the child."

One of the guys kicked her bare feet. "You think you're so smart, lady. Well, you're not. Keep your mouth shut if you know what's good for you."

Kelly obeyed.

In the corner of her eye, she could see the young British man she had befriended when he first joined the Angoon police department last year. She remembered making him feel welcome and inviting him to her church with them. He never attended, but she was always hopeful.

The man shamefully sulked in the corner. Obviously, Danny felt guilty for betraying her and was mad at her for calling him out. If she was lucky, he'd do what she said. Charlie would use up the remaining bottles by morning, and there was maybe enough formula to mix up a few more bottles tomorrow. Other than that, they were in for a big surprise. *When he's hungry, you know it!*

"I'll get some in the morning," he said, surprising her. She hadn't expected him to respond. What was he doing with these thugs anyway? "Does Boone know what you're involved with?"

"What did I tell you? Shut your gob hole!" Danny shouted from across the room. The fat one rushed up and slapped Kelly across the face then. It stung her cheek, but she tried not to cry. She focused on the baby instead. "Shhh, it's okay."

She was talking to herself mostly.

"And yes! Boone knows the plan."

WHAT ON EARTH DOES THAT MEAN?

Chocolate Bars

The night was long and cold. Kelly's feet were killing her. Not only were they cold and uncomfortable, but they were swollen under the duct tape. There was no way they could keep her ankles bound. It was too painful. She couldn't even get up to go to the bathroom properly.

It was a struggle to convince them to untie her, but she did. At least she could get up to pee now without hobbling. The weight of the babies pressing on her bladder caused her to get up several times throughout the night. Even more than Charlie.

Kelly realized the babies were not kicking as much. Her ribs didn't even hurt like they used to. In fact, she even felt smaller, like the babies had dropped between her legs like a bowling ball.

She hoped they were okay. All she could do was trust the Lord. That was *not* nothing. It was everything, actually. Kelly knew that God promised to be with her. He proved it over and over. As long as she was praying, He was staying. It's a saying she loved to repeat over and over again, reminding her that having a relationship with the Lord was the most important thing.

Sure, Kelly knew God's love wasn't dependent on her keeping her salvation, and she certainly couldn't lose it. That's not what it was all about. Even friends in her own church got confused. You don't have to earn it.

Jesus, please protect the twins, Kelly prayed silently, rubbing her huge baby bump. The cabin was dark, and two men stayed overnight to watch them. One was at the door, resting against it with a rifle. He was not sleeping. Another was snoring in a recliner.

The stroller was propped against the couch beside her, where Charlie slept, warm, dry, and fed...*for now.*

It was Lily that she worried about. They wouldn't untie her. She still sat in the same chair where they put her. They wouldn't even let her go to the bathroom. They told her they didn't trust her.

Instead, Lily peed where she sat.

A large puddle of urine had pooled under her chair. Her head hung as she slept. How could they treat a child like this? Kelly was lucky she could at least lie down to sleep. She'd have to work on them to at least let her use the bathroom properly. This was inhumane.

If they ever left, she'd try to get Lily free. It was easy enough to cut duct tape off if you had a knife, but a small manicuring scissors would have to do. She knew there was one kicking around in the diaper bag somewhere.

Hopefully, she'd find some socks as well. The last time she used the diaper bag, she ripped off her socks and shoes and stuffed them into the bottom carriage compartment under the camo baby carrier she bought for Lily.

That day, it was so warm that she had to change into her flip-flops. It was several days ago, but she hoped they were still in there somewhere. She never cleaned the thing out. This time it would pay off.

As the sun came up, Charlie started to stir. He needed a change and a bottle again. It was the last one. After this, she'd have to mix some more up. There was no real way to wash the bottles, so she'd have to improvise.

"Better take care of the brat," the voice at the door told her. "I don't want to hear him cry again."

"That's what babies do," she snapped back. She had no more patience for the fat man. He was ignorant most of the time.

"Shut up!"

Kelly obeyed.

The man in the recliner woke up then. He eased himself up from the chair and went over to check on Lily. He lifted her head and slapped her out of a sound sleep. "Wake up!" he told her. "Time to clean up. We've got some important visitors coming, and we don't need them seeing you like this."

"Hey, bro, you're not getting soft on me, are you? Just leave her the way she is. Danny will be back in a couple of hours with the supplies. We'll make Mama bear clean everything up since she wanted the job so badly."

Kelly glared at him. If he wanted her to get down on her hands and knees and scrub the floor, he had another thing coming. Yet, she figured she didn't have much of a choice.

Unless they could escape first.

If the two men would only leave the cabin for a few minutes, she could find the scissors and start whittling away at Lily's restraints. But first, she had to feed and change the baby.

She sat up, reached for the last bottle and set it in the warmer, noting the battery needed to be recharged soon. *Great!* That wasn't going to last either. The beep told her the formula was warm, so she reached for the child and scooped him up into her arms.

Kelly leaned back into the cushions of the couch and gave Charlie his bottle. He sucked like a pro. For a moment, she forgot where she was. She thought of her own twins. She'd be feeding them like this soon.

Hopefully!

They needed an escape plan, and fast. Once she got the baby changed and fed, she'd search for the scissors, even if the men were still here. *Lord Jesus, let them go outside for a bit.*

Lily looked at Charlie and whimpered. Tears filled her eyes again. She had cried most of the evening last night. They even taped her mouth shut because she wouldn't stop. Kelly tried to calm her down, but it was like she was in another world. Who knew what torture they had put her through leading up to this. No doubt she was experiencing flashbacks.

"Get your hands off me," she moaned on and off through the night, even though nobody was touching her. She probably remembered what they did to her before. Poor thing. There was no way Kelly was going to let that happen to her again.

"Hey, Sweetie," Kelly whispered to her, but the girl just glared and growled through the duct tape. "Sorry... I mean, *Lily*...I need you to stop."

She scooted over to the end of the couch, with the baby in her arms, and leaned over to whisper, "Don't let them get the best of you."

"Mmmm!" was all Lily could say.

"Listen," Kelly leaned in even closer. Both men were watching her, so she had to be careful. "I have a plan to get us out of here."

Lily's eyes grew wide. She nodded her head and looked toward the fat guy who was storming over to them now.

"Cut it out!" he slapped the back of Kelly's head. "No talking. You sit by the stroller, or else I'll tie you up again! You hear me?"

Kelly scooted her bum over. She got back to the stroller at the other end of the couch, and the fat brother headed back to the door with a rifle in hand. She winked at Lily. Then she nodded at her when he wasn't looking, mentally telling her they were going to get out of there!

Hopefully, it was the truth, because if it backfired, that was the end of it. *Lord, help us! We need a miracle right now!*

The baby finished the bottle, and she wrapped him around her shoulder and patted his back. In the meantime, she perfected the plan. First, as soon as Charlie was safe in his stroller again, she'd rummage around to find her socks and shoes from a few days ago.

Kelly decided she would use the rest of the formula she had left and mix up as many bottles as she could, even if she reused them. She'd make an excuse that she had to rinse them out at the sink. Meanwhile, she'd take a peek through the kitchen window to see if she could figure out where they were. She'd pack the diaper bag with diapers, a warmer, and bottles, and leave the stroller. As soon as the men stepped outside, she could free Lily. The girl could wear the baby in the carrier.

She was hoping for a miracle here because right now, she had no idea how this was going to work. Kelly looked around as she set the baby down in the stroller. She rummaged around and finally found her socks and shoes and put them on her cold feet. The warmth was indescribable.

"Hey! Cut it out!" the fat guy said, noticing her sudden movement.

"I found my socks and shoes. I'm just putting them on my cold feet. I'm sure you can understand. It's chilly in here since the wood stove died down."

"Lady, you talk too much."

Kelly had to de-escalate the situation quickly. She darted her eyes over to Lily as if to say she's got it under control. But really, she didn't. She'd have to appease the man somehow.

"Are you hungry?" She asked him.

"Why? You got something in that stroller to eat?" The man perked up, completely forgetting about the shoe situation. *Thank you, Lord.*

"I have four extra-large chocolate bars. You can have them all, but I need a favour in return. I need to use the sink. I have to wash the baby bottles out and mix up new formula. It will only take me a few minutes."

"Fine! Just hand over the chocolate bars."

Kelly grabbed the bars, eased her aching body up and waddled them over to the man. She then grabbed the diaper bag and headed to the sink. She moved as fast as she could to rinse the bottles, measure, and shake up the powder. In a hurry, she recapped them and stuffed them back into the bag.

She looked over at the man chomping on the chocolate bars by the door. He gave one to his brother, and they both became preoccupied while she went back to the stroller. She quickly made sure the diaper bag was stocked with diapers, sleepers, and, of course, the warmer.

Kelly made a mental note to make sure she breastfed her babies when they arrived. This formula prep was for the birds.

Thankfully, they didn't notice her checking everything

over. They were set to go, as long as she could get Lily free. They would escape at the first opportunity. Kelly hoped it was soon, because she feared that Danny would arrive soon, and so would the buyers.

While the brothers were still chewing, Kelly thoroughly searched through the stroller pockets and the diaper bag once more. She knew there was a little scissors somewhere. *Where was it?*

Then, deep in the front pocket of the diaper bag, she found it. It was a small scissors beside a miniature nail clippers. She took them both and shoved them in her shoe as she sat sideways on the couch.

"What are you doing?" the fat guy asked her, licking chocolate off his lips. He stood up and walked over to her, pointing the rifle at her belly. "Don't think I won't do it, lady. If you try anything, I'll shoot those things in your belly."

"Bro! You can't do that. They're already sold, and so is she?"

"Shut your mouth, you idiot."

Kelly gasped. No way was that happening. They needed to leave, now! She looked over at Lily. There was nothing but sorrow in her eyes.

Then a loud muffler broke the silence. The truck was back. Kelly realized this was their only shot. The two men rushed outside, leaving them alone in the cabin.

"We have to hurry," she told Lily. Jumping into action immediately. She cut through the duct tape on Lily's feet first. Then her hands, then the chair. She ripped off the tape from her mouth, all while watching the door.

"Get up, Lily! GET UP!

The girl moved like a turtle but slowly got up. Kelly grabbed the diaper bag and baby carrier and handed them to Lily. "Carry it!"

She scooped Charlie into her arms and headed for the front door. Hopefully, they would be able to slip out unnoticed. She cracked the door open and saw them all in a huddle by the black truck in the distance. Thankfully, it was foggy.

"Stay close to me."

Lily followed like a toddler. She didn't say a word.

The two of them slid sideways out the cracked door. Kelly quietly closed it behind them. They were outside. They shimmied along the rough spruce wall until they reached the opposite side of the cabin.

The three of them slipped silently into the fog.

The Handshake

Boone decided to skirt the perimeter of Angoon first before doing anything else. His uncle's expensive camouflaged hunting gear made him nearly invisible in the tree line. That's why he headed there. He also took his uncle's crossbow because it was silent, but he decided to take one of the handguns Aunt Sally had in the house, as well as two knives. One on his belt, and one strapped to his right calf under his pant leg.

He was prepared.

Now all he had to do was find his wife. He'd start with the obvious. He lay on the forest floor at the top of a hill overlooking the town, peering through a pair of high-powered binoculars. Even though there was fog, it was patchy, and he was still able to see what he needed to see. He wasn't quite close enough to see the harbour, but it was a start.

Everyone coming in and out of Angoon came in through the harbour. Rarely would anyone come across land. He knew the terrain was much too difficult to go by foot or ATV. Boone knew this firsthand when they got lost after the plane crash before he and Kelly got married. They were still dealing with the trauma from that fateful adventure.

It was better left in a distant memory.

From his vantage point, he could see the police station. That's what he wanted to see first. He could see John talking to Danny. That wasn't unusual. The two had become pretty close lately. Boone figured it was because of the plan that was now irrelevant. He wondered what exactly would happen now.

Hopefully, John had a backup plan. It made him sick what was happening. All that work to prepare for this one operation, and it had gone right out the window. It didn't matter now. He wasn't part of their group, and he didn't care. They didn't have his back. They couldn't protect his wife, and he wanted to know why. How on earth did Jimmy get to Kelly without them knowing it?

And where was Jimmy, anyway? Boone knew he had to be somewhere. He could see the old Halloway house from where he was. They rented it the last time. Would they be stupid enough to rent it again? Sure enough, Boone could see someone moving around on the property. He didn't look like his ex-buddy with fishing gear on, but that didn't mean he wasn't wearing a disguise. Why would he show up wearing his usual biker black, gang insignia, anyway? That would be stupid.

It was probably him, but Boone had to get a closer look.

Before he headed down to the harbour, he decided to take a moment to pray. He bowed his head and asked God to protect his wife, Lily, and Charlie. He asked the Lord to guide his steps and help him find them, and to protect them all from Jimmy. He was the real threat. He was a wild card. He always was.

Boone remembered getting sucked in by him all those years ago, when he made a mistake and trusted him. "Just fly my stolen goods to Anchorage. It's easy money," Jimmy told him that fateful day. Well, there was nothing easy about it. It ended in a prison sentence, and he lost everything he ever had. It was a hard-core lesson that almost cost him his life as well. Looking back now, it wasn't what he lost, but what he gained that was most important. He realized that if it hadn't been for the mistake he made that sent him to prison, he never would have found the Lord, Jesus Christ.

That put a smile on his face. *Thank you, Jesus!*

Boone wondered what good could come from this horrible situation. Kelly was so vulnerable. Anything could happen to her or the babies. One wrong move, and Jimmy could destroy his entire family. He knew the guy was capable of doing that.

Jimmy had stories so wild, they made him cringe when

he told them. When Boone first met him, he thought he was making it up, but he wasn't. At least not from what he could tell. The guy was as wild as they come. He figured he must be psychotic or something. It was like he didn't have a conscience.

At first, hanging out with him was fun. His wild side was exciting, and Boone enjoyed the craziness. Then the guy started bringing home strays and torturing them with his knives he wheeled around all the time. It turned his stomach. He told the guy that if he kept doing that kind of stuff, he wouldn't hang out with him. He stopped for a while, at least in front of him.

Then he started some other weird stuff. Often, he told Boone stories about the ex-girlfriends he tortured. He didn't believe him until one day he came over to visit him and witnessed it firsthand. One of his girlfriends fled the house, just as he arrived. The horror in her eyes told it all. Her bare arms were cut up and bleeding, as well as her cheek. Enough was enough. Boone told the guy that if he ever did it again, he'd disown him.

Well, Boone should have disowned him right then and there. But the guy had a weird way of sucking you right back into his mess. He knew now that Jimmy was probably evil. He learnt from his pastor that the guy was likely demon possessed, and to have nothing to do with him if he ever came calling again.

When he met him the last time, Boone could feel something evil right away. His discernment told him to run, but he was trapped. He didn't have a choice but to fall into the deception again.

Whether Jimmy knew he was on the up and up about joining their gang or not, it didn't matter. The guy was a danger to him and his family. Getting exposed to their dirty human trafficking ring was Jimmy's attempt at pulling him back in, except this time, Boone knew better. This time, he had God on his side. He was protected.

"You're a child of the King. The devil can't touch you," His aunt would say.

As much as he realized he was protected because he had

God on his side, he knew sin was still running rampant in the world. He had to put on God's armour and stand on guard against evil. That meant making wise decisions. One of them was quitting the detachment. He still wrestled with that one, though. He wondered if he should still check in with John. He was the police chief after all. He could probably use the guy's expertise.

Something didn't sit right with him, though. The moment those thoughts entered his mind, he got a feeling he should search for Kelly alone. *Okay, God, I'll listen.*

Boone realized, not listening to the urge of the Holy Spirit usually ended up getting him into some sort of hot water, whether that be with Kelly, his business, or something else. *Okay, God. You got my attention. I'll do what you want.*

I'll go it alone.

Boone wondered what God was up to. Just when he couldn't possibly endure one more hardship, something like this happened. How could God use this and turn it around for His good? It was unimaginable. Maybe he could put Jimmy away for life. Maybe he could help protect innocent children in the future, maybe even his own. Maybe that's what this was all about.

He realized even though the plan he and the detachment had trained for all these weeks had fallen through, he still had a mission to do. Maybe even more meaningful and impacting than the original plan.

As he climbed down the embankment that led to the harbour, he ducked down when he saw the familiar faces he was looking for. It was, in fact, Jimmy. Boone hid behind some trees and used his binoculars again. He could see the tall fella he had met at the Halloway house three months ago, when they were first in Angoon. Another man walked up the dock to greet them, and Jimmy and the tall man shook hands. It looked like the new stranger had just flown in by seaplane.

The ring leader, maybe?

Boone watched intently through the binoculars. Jimmy was wearing fishing gear, and the tall guy was as well. A disguise? Maybe. All he knew was it looked like a business deal. That's exactly what it was.

Then, a police car rolled up. *It was about time,* Boone thought. The good-for-nothing police force had better step in and do something before these guys harm anyone else. Yet, he wondered what the police could do at this point. Wasn't it premature? Why would they step in now, before they even exposed the crime?

Boone observed what was going on. It was a transaction all right. The stranger handed Jimmy and the tall man a suitcase, and all in front of an Angoon police officer. He figured this had likely happened many times before. No wonder there were reports of girls going missing all over Alaska lately.

Then, Danny got out of the car. He wasn't even inconspicuous. It was broad daylight, and he went right up to the guys. That wasn't part of the plan. How could the man be so stupid? Didn't they want to catch them red-handed first? What on earth was this kind of policing anyway?

He could see Danny talking to them. Then he shook Jimmy's hands, as well as the tall man's hand, and the stranger's hand as well. It was like they were old buddies. What on earth was going on here?

Was he in on it?

I Told You So

Kelly and Lily snuck into the bushes nearby. The fog didn't last very long, but at least it camouflaged them until they got to safety. They could still see the cabin, and the men were talking beside the truck. They only had minutes to get as far away as they could.

"Here, put this on," Kelly tried to strap the baby carrier to Lily. "You're going to have to carry Charlie. Can you do that? *Lily?*"

The girl was in a daze. She seemed traumatized by what had happened to her. If she couldn't get Lily to snap out of it, they were in trouble. Kelly couldn't do this alone, not while big and pregnant. There was no way she was strapping a baby carrier onto her belly.

Kelly tried another way. She grabbed the girl's hand and prayed. *"Lord Jesus, right now, Lily needs your help. She's been through so much, and she's having a hard time. Can you please heal her aching heart and help her save her child?"*

Tears rolled down Lily's bruised and bloodied cheeks. She nodded her head and didn't say a word. Instead, she helped Kelly get the carrier on and placed the sleeping baby inside. It was only a matter of time before Charlie woke up and wanted to be fed. Then, his crying would give them away for sure.

Once Charlie was loaded into the carrier and Lily was ready to go, Kelly tightened her housecoat around the flimsy nightgown she had on from the day before, and flung the diaper bag over her shoulder. Thankfully, she had shoes, but her bare legs felt like they were on fire exposed to the cold November morning. It seemed like the heat wave was over. Temperatures had plummeted overnight, and that didn't run in their favour.

Now, where should they go?

Kelly looked in all directions. There were no paths to follow. It was solid underbrush. All she could see was wall-to-wall spruce trees and thick underbrush. She couldn't even tell which way was north. She didn't want to go that way, nor did she want to go east. She and Boone got lost that way when they met up with the Kushtaka several years ago. Neither one of them had been there since.

Lord, make a way. Please!

All Kelly knew was that she had to lead them away from the cabin. If the sun rose against their backs, that meant they'd be going west. That should lead them back to town, that is, if they could find a way through the underbrush.

As they pushed through the forest, slapping against spruce branches, Kelly discovered an old trap line. It looked abandoned, but she could still see the old path it followed. Boone showed her these kinds of things in their first year of marriage. He wanted to teach her how to survive in the bush after their devastating plane crash. He told her it was a valuable skill. "You never know when you're going to need survival skills," he told her.

He was right.

Kelly grabbed Lily's hand and the two of them pushed through to the trap line. They swatted against prickly branches and carefully maneuvered over moss and dead tree stumps. Charlie still slept quietly in the baby carrier strapped to his mother.

The sun was high enough above them to tell Kelly it was around noon. Charlie still hadn't woken up yet, but she knew it was only a matter of time. Once he did, they'd have to stop somewhere to give him a bottle. She looked around for a comfortable spot.

They were making good time. She hadn't heard anything from the valley below where the cabin was. All she heard was the echo of vehicle doors slamming about half an hour ago. They sped off down a road that led the other way. Kelly didn't really care where they were, as long as they didn't come after them. She figured they were too lazy to head into the bush. They didn't seem the survival type. More like the kind that wasted hours and hours playing video games.

"I think we'll stop here," she told Lily. "My side is aching so bad coming up this hill. I can't go any further. How are you doing?"

Lily said, "Okay." She was finally talking. She spoke a word here and there, but frankly, Kelly was worried about her. She still wasn't talking in complete sentences.

"How long has your side been hurting?" The girl asked her abruptly. Kelly was surprised so many words came out of her mouth, but she was glad to hear them. Maybe this meant the girl was finally coming around.

"I got elbowed in the side pretty hard when they took me. It's been aching ever since," she answered the girl. "Going up this hill has only made it worse."

"How worse?"

Kelly looked at her as she stood there. "Why do you ask?"

"Because I know."

"What do you know?"

"How it feels to have a baby."

Kelly felt shivers go up her spine. This is not what was happening. These babies were not ready to come out yet. They still had to cook for a few more weeks. It was only her side aching because they had elbowed her so hard.

"I'm sure you know how it feels, but it's not time for the babies to come out yet."

"Okay." The girl shrugged and kept going uphill.

"Stop! Lily, I told you I can't go any further."

"Fine then! Admit that I know a little something about this." The girl stood there with her hands on her hips, matter-of-factly.

Kelly did not need this attitude, but she was a teenager, after all: A teenager with a baby. A baby who was suddenly waking in his carrier. Lily looked at him and stuffed his soother in his mouth. Then she continued, "Well? Admit it!"

"Okay, fine! I'm sorry. You obviously know more than me about this than I do. You birthed a baby. But Lily, I'm not in labour. I'm just tired."

"And...you have pains. I've been watching you. They come in waves, on and off like someone's turning a switch. That's what happened to me, but I didn't know what it was. Trust me, it's labour."

"No, it is not!"

"Yes, it is!"

It was pointless to argue, especially in this situation. They were both exhausted. Kelly knew it wasn't labour, but there was no convincing the girl. She'd just leave it alone. They had more important things to worry about right now. Besides, labour didn't feel like side cramps. She was sure of it. From what she read, you get squeezing pains in the front of your stomach every couple of minutes.

"Look, let's not argue. I appreciate your concern, but I'm fine. Now, let's sit down in this moss for a bit and feed Charlie. We can both rest, and then we'll head up there," she pointed to the top of the ridge. From up there, they could get a better vantage point and hopefully see the town.

Lily shrugged and headed to the moss. Kelly helped her loosen the baby carrier and then pull Charlie out. She grabbed a baby blanket from the diaper bag and tossed it to the girl. She quickly wrapped the baby and held him tight.

Kelly grabbed a bottle from the bag and put it in the bottle warmer. "Battery low," it said. She bit her lip and pressed start anyway. Within a few minutes, Charlie was chugging it down. "He's a hungry little guy."

Lily just looked at her and shrugged.

"Look, I didn't mean to imply that you don't know what you're talking about. I know you do. You birthed this little guy. You know how it feels. You went through a lot of trauma, and you know what it's like to have a child come out of you."

"He came out into the toilet. If I had known what was happening, I would have lain down. I wish someone had helped me."

"And that's why you want to help me, isn't it?" Kelly sighed. "I'm sorry."

"You'll be sorry when those babies pop out in a bush somewhere."

"Oh, they will not. C'mon, Lily, stop it!"

The girl shrugged again and went silent.

Kelly knew she was not in labour. All that was wrong with her was that she had to go to the bathroom pretty badly. These babies were sitting right on her bladder. She had to go several times on the way through the bush. She didn't think she had any more pee in her. She wasn't even drinking anything.

"I gotta pee," Kelly told Lily. "That's all that's wrong with me." She slowly lifted her belly first, and then her legs followed. "Oh, that hurts." She paused as she finally got to her feet. Then more pain came on. This time it was her back. Still not her stomach, so she was fine. Lily was not right.

"See," the girl defended her stance. "Every twenty minutes or so, you get a pain. I do have a watch, you know."

Kelly shook her head and laughed as she headed to a bush to relieve herself. Anyone would be tired and achy in her condition if they just trudged up a hill in dense forest. She refused to put that thought into her head. After all, truth be told, she had pains every day. At this point, everything ached all the time.

As Kelly looked around to make sure she had privacy, she slid her underpants down and urinated into the moss. What a relief. Now she could function again. Part of the problem was that she felt like she had to go every twenty minutes. That's the only thing that seemed to bother her. Not the pain. It was alarming, yes, but it wasn't labour.

Then, as she got up, she spotted blood in the moss. She wiped with her hand, and there was more blood. There wasn't a lot of it, but enough to tell her something was wrong. It brought back painful memories of the miscarriages.

No, she was almost nine months pregnant. There was no risk of that anymore. Not like before. Surely, it was just part of being in her third trimester. She pulled up her underwear, straightened herself out, and pulled her housecoat over her belly.

No, this was nothing at all.

Then, as she walked back to Lily, stumbling over a stump, she realized she hadn't stopped peeing yet. She was still going. It was gushing down her leg. This was not good. She bent over to see, and it wasn't blood. It was mostly pee. Her water couldn't have broken yet. It was way too early.

When she came back to Lily and the baby, they were still on the ground feeding. Lily looked up and smiled when another pain hit. This time, it hit hard. Kelly bent over and used a tree to support herself while moaning.

"See…I told you so. You're in labour."

146

Piggyback

The seagulls were crying overhead as they circled Boone's boat. He snuck down to the harbour where it was docked and decided to hide inside to watch the men. He couldn't find the hidden key, so he decided to jump aboard and look for the emergency spare.

It wasn't unusual for Lily to play on the boat. She probably lost the spare. He knew about her going down to the boat for a long time now, but said nothing. It wasn't a big deal anyway. If the girl needed some space, he wanted to give her that. As long as she didn't try to go anywhere with it, it was fine.

However, now that the key was missing, he had to find the emergency one he kept on deck. He snuck to the bow of the ship and fingered through the lip of the railing. There it was. He unlocked the door and quickly slipped inside. Through his binoculars, he peered at the group of men at the other end of the dock and observed them. They all boarded a lime green schooner, including Danny.

After about twenty minutes, they left the boat and got into the police cruiser together. Danny drove, still in uniform, still on duty. That angered Boone, but there was nothing he could do for now. He'd wait for them to leave and then break into the boat and snoop around. Thankfully, there weren't a lot of people on the dock yet, and he could get over there without being noticed.

Boone climbed on board the old wooden lime green schooner and picked the lock to the cabin. It was a skill he was not proud of, but thankful for. He was surprised that he still remembered how to do it after being taught the art of it in prison.

Thank you, Shane. He never thought he'd thank the good-for-nothing bum for anything. Boone shook his head and went inside. Right away, he could smell the rank smell on board. It smelled like body odour and feces. That alarmed him. The pungent smell was too much for his nose. He'd have to work quickly.

First, he looked around for a map. Perhaps he could figure out where they were headed or where they came from. If the plan was to take Lily, he wanted to know where. He'd have to do things his own way and call the coast guard after this. If Danny was in on it, that meant he'd have to go over the heads of the Angoon police department.

Boone remembered the old plan, and even after all the details were finalized, he wondered why the Coast Guard was never made a part of it. If the crime was happening by boat or seaplane, wouldn't that be their jurisdiction?

He always scratched his head on this one, but what did he know? He was just a new trainee peace officer. An ex officer now. And there was a lot he didn't know. But since he saw Danny with them, there was nowhere else to turn but the Coast Guard.

He reached into his pocket for his cell phone and pulled it out. He'd call now, before this whole thing got any worse. In a hurry, Boone went to dial the number, but noticed he had 1% battery power left. He'd need a charger for it first, and that would be impossible. He left his at home, in his burnt house. Either he'd have to find one on board, or go back to his own boat, where he knew he had a spare.

Then, from below, Boone suddenly heard a sound.

"Hello?"

Boone went below to see, figuring it was a cat or something that knocked over a dish from the rocking motion of the ocean waves. It wasn't unheard of, but being that it was calm waters right now, it didn't make it likely.

Then he heard it again. It was a distinct knocking sound. He forged through the belly of the boat until he got to a closet.

It was then that he heard a faint whimper. Someone was locked inside. Was it Lily?

Again, a whimper and a kick.

The closet had a padlock on it, but thankfully, Boone could pick it. He grabbed the bobby pins he got from Aunt Sally, and broke open the lock, revealing a very young girl inside. She whimpered even louder.

"It's okay! I'm here to help you."

The girl whimpered and withdrew. She was afraid of him. She walked away from him and started crying. Her mouth was bound with a rage pulled tightly around her face. It was bloody and bruised, and her straight blonde hair was matted with blood. Both feet were tied together, as were her wrists.

Not Lily!

This girl looked like she was nothing more than twelve years old. She was skinny with a slight build. She trembled and whimpered as she kicked at him with her soiled red running shoes.

"I won't hurt you. I'm here to help."

The girl looked wide-eyed at him then, and stopped whimpering. She held her wrists up for him to cut the rope.

Boone reached under his right pant leg and took out his hunting knife. He sawed through the rope and freed her hands, then he cut through the ankle rope. She pulled off her mouth gag and said, "Hurry, they're coming back."

"They're gone for now. I saw them leave."

"NO! THEY'RE COMING BACK!"

Boone could see the fear in her eyes. He helped her out of the closet, but she could barely walk. He turned around. "Here, hop on! I'll give you a piggyback."

The little girl trembled and jumped up, holding on to his neck. He pushed forward through the mess down below and headed up the stairs. Boone figured he'd take her to Aunt Sally. Nobody knew she was in the church dorm where he told her to wait for him. He couldn't take her to the police station. He didn't trust it. And he couldn't take her to his boat. It was only a matter of time before Jimmy found out which boat was his.

If he didn't know it already.

As Boone surfaced to the deck of the boat, he spotted a map and paused to look at it. Someone had circled North Head Lighthouse. *Washington?* Was that the next pickup point? Or maybe a drop off?

This was going to end now! He'd take the girl to Aunt Sally, charge his phone and call the Coast Guard. Now all he had to do was get there.

"Hurry!" The girl cried. They're coming back!" Boone moved as fast as he could. "It's okay, sweetheart. I got you!"

Lord, God Almighty, help me get her to safety!

Eating Crow

It was a slug, but Boone finally made it to where his Aunt Sally was staying. The little girl nearly broke his back, but he didn't mind. At least she was safe, for now. He made sure nobody saw him carrying the girl on his back.

"Oh, for heaven's sake," Aunt Sally groaned when she saw him. "Come inside, quickly!" She looked both ways before shutting the door. "And who is this?"

"What's your name, darling?" Boone asked her out of breath. He put the trembling child down. She didn't speak.

"You're safe now!" Boone told her. He helped the child to the couch and motioned for his aunt to talk to him in private. They went into the kitchen and whispered out of earshot of the girl.

"What is going on, Boone? Look at her!"

"I know. She was kidnapped, just like Lily."

"What? Lily?" His aunt's eyes went wide. She didn't know any of this. It was the first time he could actually tell his aunt what was going on. Right now, he wished he had done it earlier. He wished he had been able to tell his wife. John didn't want him to. He said that would put them in danger, yet it happened anyway.

"Lily was kidnapped before she had Charlie. I wasn't supposed to tell anyone, but these guys are in town now, including my ex-buddy, Jimmy. I found the girl on their boat."

"What? You don't make sense. Slow down!"

"I can't, Aunt Sally. I gotta go find Kelly, now! I need you to charge my cell phone. I have to call the Coast Guard."

"What? Why not call John? I know he's incompetent, but

he is your friend."

Boone cringed. Maybe he should. Maybe he should swallow his pride and ask John for help, after all. Especially now with a young girl involved. She needed medical attention. She was in danger, and so were Kelly and Lily.

What do I do, Lord?

It was a hard decision, but Boone decided he had to talk to John first, even though his gut told him not to. Maybe his frustration with quitting was all he was feeling. Aunt Sally made sense. "Fine, I'll stop by the detachment. But if I get the vibe that something's wrong, I do it my way again."

"Your way is fine," Aunt Sally told him. "But just go talk to him first. I think you need some help. Anyone who would do this to a little girl is a monster. That means, Kelly and Lily and Charlie are in real danger."

"I told you that. That's why I can't stay. Charge my phone and I'll be back for it. I'll go talk to John and see what I can find out."

"I don't have a charger. I lost my phone. I'd have to go back to my house for it."

"And the Pastor doesn't have one kicking around?"

"No, I looked. And there's no landline either. Oh, I'm no help to you at all.

"Don't say that, Aunt Sally! "You're more of a help to me than those fools on the force have been. Danny is in on it."

"What? NO!"

"YES!" Boone told her. "Anyway, just stay here. I'll take the phone with me and get it charged somehow. You and the girl stay here. I won't tell anyone you're here. Not even John. Not yet, anyway. Not until I find out what he knows."

They went back into the living room where they had left the girl. She was lying down, crying, holding her stomach. "I don't feel so good."

"Honey! I'm gonna get you all cleaned up. I used to be a nurse, you know," Aunt Sally soothed her. Boone was thankful for the woman. He could always count on her.

Boone hugged his aunt and headed out the door. He knew the child was in good hands. Now he could focus on finding his wife. If he had to go back to the detachment, he would. Even if it was just to check in with John about how it was going. Maybe it wasn't as bad as he thought. Maybe they already found Kelly and Lily. It wasn't likely, but it was a possibility. Maybe there was even an explanation for Danny's odd behaviour.

As Boone walked through the neighbourhood, he still tried to conceal himself. He went through the alleys as much as possible, hiding behind garbage cans and outbuildings until he reached the police station. He hid behind an old shed and looked through the binoculars again. Was the coast clear? Did he see Danny and Jimmy anywhere? All he could see was John's police cruiser.

He was there.

Eating crow was not Boone's specialty. He had to swallow his pride to walk back in there after he just quit. It was hard, but he knew he had to do it if he wanted answers. *Lord, help me. I don't want to talk to the man, but I don't see any other way.*

"Boone!" The over-friendly voice shot at him. John had spotted him already, just as he came through the door. "We've been looking everywhere for you. Looks like you've been out hunting. You didn't go rogue on me, did you?"

The man was acting weird. First, Boone wondered why he didn't seem more upset. If someone quit on him, he'd still be steaming. But then, after all that had happened, maybe the guy had a heart after all.

"I've been looking into things on my own. What do you know about Danny?"

"What about him? He's a new rookie. He's okay."

"He's not okay. I saw him with Jimmy."

"What?"

"Yah! I don't think we can trust him."

Boone could tell the man was genuinely interested in what he had to say. Maybe John didn't actually know what was going on. Maybe he could trust him after all. They had been friends for quite a while now, and that had to stand for something.

"Well...I had my suspicions about the guy. I was trying to get close to him, but you know, Danny. He's a brick wall. Can't even get through the front door."

"You think he knows where Kelly is?"

John scratched his nose and cleared his throat. "Actually, since you've been out playing the hero, we managed to track Kelly and Lily down. The group of guys in town happen to be the ones we're after. We think they're connected with this whole thing. And Jimmy. We followed them to an abandoned trapper's cabin about thirty miles northeast of town. Boone, the girls are there."

"WHAT? Are they okay?"

"Yes!" John told him. "My men have them surrounded. There are two guys inside. Looks like Kelly and Lily are tied up. Boone, they have Charlie, too."

"Oh, man!" Boone's head was spinning.

"I was headed out there now. They don't make a move until I say so."

"Well, what are we waiting for? Take me with you!"

"I was just about to ask. You up for it, bud?"

"ABSOLUTELY!"

Scaring Me

The pains kept coming, one after another. It wasn't letting up. Lily wasn't much help, but at least Charlie was sleeping again after they fed and changed him. He was back in his mother's carrier, strapped to her chest.

"We have to try to get to the top," Kelly told Lily. If they were going to flag someone for help, it would be from up there, at the top of the ridge. They could make a signal fire and hope the right people saw it first.

Thank you, Boone, for the survival teachings.

Kelly didn't know how long she had, but from the way she was feeling, it wasn't long. She was not going to give birth by herself to premature twins in the bush successfully, that was for sure. She figured they had another half hour before they reached the top.

"I'm not going up there!" Lily told her point-blank, "And neither are you! You can't walk with a baby between your legs, trust me. I know!"

"I can, and I WILL!"

"You're nuts!"

"I may be nuts, but I know how to survive in the bush. That's something you've never experienced before, my dear! We have to get to the top of the ridge. Trust me on that one. It's the only way. We need a signal fire, and nobody is going to see it where we're at."

"And you know how to make a fire without matches?"

"As a matter of fact, yes, I do! You can thank Boone for that! He drilled it into me!"

Lily smiled, "I bet he did. I can see him now. "'*You gotta do it this way! You gotta do it that way!"'* The girl mimicked her stern husband. It was funny, and Kelly was thankful for the distraction from yet another contraction. She paused and moaned until it passed.

"Okay... that was a strong one."

"I told you. It feels like you're gonna die."

Yes, Kelly was realizing that now, but one thing was for sure: they were going to die if they didn't get help soon. Not only was hypothermia a real threat out there, but she knew what lived in the bush. Bears and wolves were everywhere. There was no telling where they were prowling, and she didn't want to wait around to find out.

"Okay, let's go." Kelly grabbed a tree branch and used it for a cane. Lily did the same. Thankfully, Charlie was content and didn't make a sound. They forged upward, pressing through the underbrush as best as they could under the circumstances. The top of the ridge looked a million miles away.

It was times like this that Kelly needed her heavenly father to carry her. God had never let her down before, and she knew he would not let her down now. *"God...ME!* She prayed silently. *"I need you to somehow carry me up this hill. I can barely walk. My cramping back and belly feel like they're on fire. I NEED YOU TO HELP ME!"*

Kelly knew the only way was to keep talking to her Saviour. He was their only hope. She wished Lily would understand that. The girl wouldn't listen. No matter how hard she tried to give her the gospel, she rejected it every time. Maybe some people were not meant to be Christians, or maybe there was some other way to reach her. If there was, she apparently didn't know it. Everything she said either came out wrong or was taken the wrong way. *"Lord, please help me with that too."*

Then, Lily spoke up as if she could hear her thoughts. "I know you're praying. I can hear you whispering under your breath. Why do you even bother?"

"Because God is everything to me."

"Why?"

Kelly was thankful for the door God gave her. She prayed for it, so now she had to use it, even if another contraction was coming on hard and fast. She stopped and moaned as the pains crushed her back. She leaned on her cane for support until it finally passed.

"See...We're not gonna make it," the girl huffed. "You'd better stop!"

"WE KEEP GOING!"

Kelly composed herself and pushed upward. Thankfully, it wasn't a steep incline, but even a gradual one was difficult for a woman in labour. Regardless, she was going to continue, not only the journey, but the conversation Lily started as well.

"You asked me why God is everything to me. I want to answer that."

"Okay, but you guys have all tried, and I just don't see it your way. If there really was a God, he wouldn't have let this happen to us. He wouldn't have let me go through hell. I didn't deserve what happened to me. You know that, right?"

Again, Kelly was reminded of her atheist way of thinking. The only way through to her would be visible proof. That was few and far between, but using herself as an example had proven to be effective before. She'd at least try again.

"I know you didn't deserve what happened to you. We don't deserve what's happening right now. Nobody does. But if you think God is the one who did this, you are sadly mistaken. He didn't cause this, *the devil did.*"

"Oh, that again. Don't blame it on an equally fictitious thing. There is no devil either."

Kelly sighed. She didn't know if she wanted to have this conversation right now. It required more energy than she had right now, yet God presented the opportunity. She wanted to pursue it. *Lord, give me strength, then.*

Show her! Kelly heard a whisper in her spirit.

"Look," Kelly stopped and leaned against her cane. "Look at my scars. You say there is no devil, well, explain this!" She lifted her housecoat and nightgown to reveal her upper thigh. A horrendous claw scar revealed itself. It was something she had never shown anyone but Boone. It was from the Kushtaka. It was time to tell her what she experienced in the bush when she and Boone were attacked after their plane crash.

Though the Kushtaka legend is a Tlingit myth, she knew they were real. She experienced the attack firsthand. Like the Sasquatch legend, the Kushtaka were an otter-man-like creature very much like the Nephilim the Bible speaks about. It tried to suck her soul out of her. After the experience, she didn't speak of it again. Nobody would believe her. Only Boone, because they had been attacked together.

It was a painful trauma she and her husband shared, and something nobody would ever believe, and nobody ever wanted to. It was something they kept locked up deep inside of them. It was the reason Boone pushed her to learn survival skills. It was her rock-solid proof that the devil existed. And if the devil was real, so was God.

Not that she ever needed that kind of proof. She had faith before this experience ever happened. That's what protected them. It was those who don't believe in Jesus Christ and his finished work on the cross that the Kushtaka go after. She witnessed that first hand when a lawyer named Patrick lost his life in front of them.

Kelly had never spoken of Patrick out loud until now. Just the sound of his name coming out of her mouth sent shivers up her spine. The girl took it all in, listening to her every word. She hated that she had to bring her through this painful memory, but it was what she needed: *Proof.*

Lily needed to hear why God was everything to her. That was her *why*. She hadn't even touched on the fact that the Heavenly Father was the only real father she ever knew. He stepped in where her earthly father had failed her. One day, she'd tell her that story too.

Right now, it was time to rest again. Kelly felt another twinge coming on. She knew what that meant. The contraction overpowered her. This time, it was more intense than the last time. It nearly crushed her. It sent her down on her knees as she moaned and groaned on all fours in the moss.

"You're scaring me!" The girl cried out, "Please stop!"

Kelly tried to speak, but she couldn't move her mouth. Every ounce of energy went into coping with the intense pain. It was too much, *far too much!*

Finally, the labour pains started to subside. She sucked in a breath and tried to stand. It was more difficult than she let on, but she tried not to show it. "I'm sorry, Lily. The contractions are getting more intense. We'd better get going. We're almost at the top. I'll try not to scare you again."

"You better not! Not with that, or the stupid monster story. I know you made it up."

Kelly wanted to defend herself, but this wasn't the time or the place. She gave it her best shot. Sure, she scared her, but sometimes that's what people need. There is a God, and there is a devil. *Period!* If your soul isn't protected by the blood of Jesus Christ, then you're at risk for spiritual attacks, not to mention physical ones as well.

Kelly was glad God gave her the discernment to know this. Now, if she could only teach it to Lily. She figured that wasn't really up to her, though. It was something the Holy Spirit was in charge of. No amount of badgering would bring someone to Christ. It was a sad reality, but something she just had to accept.

Not my will, but thine be done!

How Can I Forget

Boone felt stupid for thinking his friend had his best interest at heart. He figured it out about halfway to the cabin. John abruptly stopped the car, told him to get out, and slapped handcuffs on him. He directed him by gunpoint to the back seat, locking him in the police cruiser. "Sorry, bud, but I know you."

Yeah, right!

The guy was a dirty cop. He made the mistake of trusting him. All those nights going over the plan, and not once did he mention the coast guard. His attitude toward Lily was always disrespectful, like he thought she had deserved what happened to her or something.

Why did he ever trust him to keep his family safe? He fumed in the back seat. "You're never going to get away with this, John. After all these years, what made you turn? Was it the money? Are you that shallow?"

"Shut up, or I'll shut you up!"

Boone shook his head. He wouldn't put it past the guy. He was the one with the gun. He wouldn't let Boone take his. He wouldn't even let him take the bow. "Oh, you won't need it, buddy! Let's leave it behind. My men have the place surrounded, anyway. They got the guns. Leave it to them." He even took the knife attached to his belt. Lucky for him, he still had the one strapped to his right calf. It would remain hidden under his pant leg until he needed it."

"Just answer me this," Boone ignored the guy's threat. "How long? How long have you been in on it? From the start?"

"No, not from the start. Danny made me an offer I

couldn't refuse."

"You fool! You have no idea."

"And I suppose you do?"

"I do. I only told you half of my story."

"Whatever. I think I have a little more experience than you do."

"I doubt that! You just play the part. Big man in the precinct. You think you know criminals just because you lock them up? Well, you don't. You have no idea. They eat guys like you for dinner, and then they spit out the bones."

John laughed, "You're funny. You actually believe what comes out of your mouth. These guys aren't like that. Danny filled me in before they came. The buyer even paid me my share already."

"JOHN!" Boone pleaded, "IT'S NOT TOO LATE! Just work with me. We can still get these guys. It's not worth it!"

"That's easy for you to say, you're not the one who got his pension delayed. Yeah, the budget got cut. I was supposed to retire last year, and then they told me I couldn't access it until I'm 70 years old now. I'll be dead by then."

"I'm sorry, John! I didn't know."

John bit his lip. Boone could see the man's frustration in the rear-view mirror. It was heartbreaking; he thought this was his only option. Maybe there was a way to still convince him to do the right thing. "What would Cindy have thought?"

That was obviously the wrong thing to say. John slammed on the brakes so hard that Boone nearly hit the cage that separated the front from the back. "WHAT DID YOU SAY?"

Boone was quiet. He knew he didn't like talking about his deceased wife. She passed away in a car accident last year. He knew the man still held onto the pain of it. A drunk driver clipped her SUV and sent her over the edge of a canyon. It was heartbreaking.

"YOU DON'T GET TO SAY HER NAME! She would have agreed with me, you know. The suffering I put her through all those years. You know what the force does to you? You know what it did to her? Even still, she always supported me. "'Just five more years and you'll get your pension, honey. It will be worth it, honey. Then we can travel, honey.' WELL, IT'S TOO LATE NOW, ISN'T IT! SHE'S DEAD!"

Silence filled the police cruiser after his outburst. Boone had no comeback for that. The man was distraught. He still hadn't gotten over his wife's death. His judgment was clouded with all that pain and regret.

Jesus, please comfort this man, and help him reconsider what he's doing.

As they pulled up to the abandoned trapper's cabin, Boone looked at the surroundings. All he could see was one other police cruiser. Hopefully, Kelly was okay. He wasn't sure what exactly he was walking into.

"Can you at least take off the handcuffs? Give me a fighting chance!" Boone asked his old friend. The same guy they spent holidays and Christmases with.

"They said they wouldn't hurt you. They just want to talk."

"John! They don't just want to talk!"

"Look," the guy turned around in the front seat. "This all depends on you. If you don't give them any of that bravado stuff, they said they'd let Kelly go. Just keep your mouth shut. I know that's hard for you, but just try to listen. They have an ultimatum."

I'm sure they do. Boone knew how these guys operated, especially Jimmy. There was no coming back from this. If he could play along long enough to make sure they release Kelly, that was all he could hope for.

John got out of the car and reached into the back seat to grab him. He shoved him down the path and through the front door, but he couldn't see Kelly. Danny was there, along with Jimmy and his thugs, plus a new guy.

Maybe they were keeping Kelly in another room.

"Where's my wife?" Boone blurted out.

"Well, well, well! How's my lifelong buddy?" Jimmy

smiled through rotten teeth.

"I'm not your buddy."

"Oh, that hurts. And after I trusted you and everything. Imagine my disappointment when I heard you double-crossed me. I thought we went way back. I thought you wanted to join us. You know what you are? You're a dirty rotten snitch. You know what we do to snitches, don't you?"

Boone refused to give him the satisfaction of an answer. Of course, he knew. He wasn't stupid. John was the stupid one for believing all they wanted to do was talk. That was a joke. Surely the man knew better than that.

"Guys," John spoke up, "I thought you had an ultimatum for him."

"Well, now, that would require something to trade. Unless he knows where his wife is, the deal is off, John!"

Did that mean what he thought it meant? Did Kelly and Lily escape? He hoped that's what he meant, because he refused to even entertain the alternative.

"Where's my wife?"

"Well, Boone," Jimmy came at him and punched him in the head. "YOU TELL ME! These guys came a long way for their merchandise. Now, we're willing to let your precious wife go, but one of them here is a doctor, and he's prepared to do a C-section and take those twins of yours to a buyer. The ultimatum WAS going to be that we get the infants and Lily, in exchange, we'll let you little wifey go. But not anymore, unless you're willing to cooperate and find them for us."

Boone sat on the chair they put him in. He was stunned. She did escape. And she knew the bush and how to survive in it, just like he taught her to. He wondered if he should pretend to play along with their ultimatum and find her. They were going to kill them either way, but it might buy him some time.

"We know you know the wilderness," Jimmy sneered. "Look at you, all commando and everything. Makes my heart sing. All you have to do is track her and bring them back. I know it's pretty simple for you. My guys aren't half as good as you are at trapping. They tried, but they came back empty-handed. You know what that means."

Boone knew what he meant. He killed them. He didn't even have to ask.

"Fine! I'll track her and bring her back, but how do I know you'll let her go?"

"You don't."

"You bring the girls back, or we'll kill your Aunty Sally, simple as that."

Then, from out of one of the rooms, Boone saw the horrific sight. They brought his aunt into view, beaten and bloody.

"Aunt Sally!"

"What a reunion. And the girl... well, thank you for trying to rescue her. You're such a hero. It was an added treat to find her there. She's been a real fighter, you know. We had to lock her in the closet and everything. I'm surprised to hear she behaved for you. She likes big, burly men like you. Don't you, honey."

They dragged the tiny blonde girl out of the room, kicking and screaming, then. She was all tied up, just the way Boone found her. The sight of it made him sick.

"So, you see, everyone's depending on you. I know that's how you like it, though. So, get to it. You'd better find them before it gets too dark. You've got two hours or your precious Aunt Sally dies. Got it?"

John paced behind them. Boone could tell he was itching to say something. He hoped he didn't, because these guys were not fooling around. *Shut your mouth, John!*

"Hey, guys," John interrupted, "This isn't what we talked about. Let the old woman go. I can take her back in the cruiser. She's not part of this. She's my friend. She and my wife grew up together. *PLEASE!*"

"SHUT UP, JOHN!" Boone told him.

"Oh, okay," Jimmy sneered. "So that's how it is. He's *your* buddy now. You want me to just let your lady friend go for free?

Johnny boy, you can't have something for nothing. Don't you know that by now? It's gonna cost you."

"Fine! I'll pay for her."

"Hand over the money we gave you then. *All of it!*"

"NO! Forget it. I'm only paying half."

Boone watched the bantering back and forth. He held his breath, knowing how it was going to end, hoping it wasn't true. He'd heard plenty of Jimmy's stories about scenarios like this. Whether they were true or not didn't matter; it was his fantasy, and there was no stopping that.

"Have it your way," Jimmy smiled, pointing his gun at John's head.

"No, no, no! I'll pay, I'll pay!"

"You'll pay, alright." Jimmy exploded the handgun right through John's forehead before the man even had a chance. His lifeless body crumpled to the floor with a thud. "Anyone else wanna play any games? Hugh?"

Jimmy looked around the room, reeling his gun like a madman. It sickened Boone to know what his ex-friend was capable of. Not that he didn't know it already, just that witnessing the psychopath in action meant he'd do that to his entire family in a heartbeat.

"Take my cuffs off. I'll go find the girls," Boone broke the silence.

"Now, that's my Boone dog! Remember, you have two hours."

How can I forget!

Help Me

By the time Kelly and Lily reached the clearing at the top of the ridge, it was late afternoon. They stopped a few more times to feed Charlie and change his diaper along the way. The contractions continued. They prevented them from moving as quickly as they should have, but at least they made it to the top.

It took longer to make a fire as well. Everything was slower with a baby in tow, not to mention Kelly's progressing labour. They sat on tree stumps around a fire now, feeding it with twigs and logs until it was roaring. Surely someone would spot them up there.

Kelly and Lily could see the town below, a few miles to the left. To the right, they could see the ocean and the setting sun. At least they were warm. That brought comfort. If they were stuck up there for much longer, the babies would come. That thought was frightening, but inevitable.

Someone see us.

The crackle of the fire was calming, and it helped with contractions. As each pain came, Kelly focused on the flames. They were so colourful. She hadn't noticed that before. Each flame mixed with all the different tones of yellow, orange and blue. God's creation really was beautiful. The Lord had helped them get to the top. His love was unimaginable!

Kelly wished Lily could experience that.

Lily had Charlie out of his carrier and was playing with him. She seemed distant, sitting there cooing at him. Kelly was pretty sure she was mad at her for telling her the story about the Kushtaka, but she didn't regret it one bit. The girl needed to hear it.

They were in serious trouble up there. This was no game. The only help Kelly could rely on was the Lord, Jesus Christ. He was their only hope, and she had to know that. In fact, it was time to start praying. She was doing it anyway, but now she'd do it out loud.

"Lily, let's pray. We need all the help we can get right now."

"Let's not."

"Well…you can do what you want, but I'm going to pray out loud. God's the only one that can get us out of here, and we need him right now. *I* need him right now. My contractions are really close together, and I'm starting to feel funny."

"What do you mean, feel funny?" Lily asked with a worried look on her face. "You're not giving birth right now, are you? You sound like a dead dog. I really can't stand any more of this. I never made such horrible sounds when I had Charlie. Maybe it's different when you have two babies in your belly. I'm glad I just had one kid pop out."

Kelly's head throbbed, and her eyes were blurry. Something was wrong. Her contractions were strong and hard, but now she was feeling lightheaded. Maybe this was all part of it. Maybe she should stop complaining. If a fourteen-year-old could do this, so could she. She wished the pain would stop already. Enough was enough.

"Lord Jesus," Kelly prayed aloud. *"Please help us! Please help me! These babies are coming. I don't know what to do."* Then another contraction came on, and she started praying the Lord's Prayer as she cried. *"Yea though I walk through the valley of the shadow of death, I will fear no evil, thy rod and thy staff they comfort me."*

"STOP IT!"

"I'm sorry, Lily! I can't help it!" Kelly moaned and cried loudly.

"You're scaring me. I don't know how to help you."

The baby started to cry, and Lily stood up and started rocking him. "You're even upsetting Charlie. Can't you be quiet?

This is too much! What am I supposed to do?"

Kelly tried not to let the girl's words upset her. Lily was just a child, and this had to be upsetting to her. It might even be giving her ptsd from her own experience. Still, even if she wanted to, she couldn't stop moaning. It was something she couldn't control. The more she tried, the more lightheaded she felt.

Another hard contraction hit, sending Kelly into a guttural moan. The baby cried, and so did Lily. She couldn't even think, let alone speak. It was the most intense pain she'd ever felt.

Focus! Look at the flames. See them dance. Watch their colours, yellow, orange, and blue.

The crushing pain across her middle felt like a vice grip tightening. One, two, three… she breathed out, then gasped for air, and did it all over again until it finally subsided.

It was a terrible situation, and there was no getting out of this. Either they get help soon, or she is going to have to prepare to give birth right in front of the fire. She'd have to go through the diaper bag and see what she could use. There were some sterile wipes and baby blankets she could use. She could also use her robe to wrap the babies in. It didn't matter if she was cold. Her main priority was keeping the babies as warm as possible until help arrived.

How on earth am I going to do this, Lord?

Kelly knew she had to tell Lily what to do. She needed the girls' help whether she wanted to or not. "Lily, I need you to listen to me. I need you to put Charlie back in the carrier. I can help you fasten it if you come over here. Do it quickly. I need your help."

"No! I'm not helping!"

"Lily, please!"

"I-I'm watching Charlie, that's it!"

Kelly sat on the edge of the log and held her head as she leaned forward and puked. She wiped her mouth and started to breathe heavily, feeling another contraction coming on. This time, she felt dizzy. Something was happening, and it was out of her control.

Lily put the baby in the carrier across her chest and came over to get Kelly to help her buckle the straps. With a shaky hand, she helped the girl. At least Charlie was safe. Now all she had to do was get the girl to assist with the birth.

Except…she felt faint.

Lord Jesus! Help! The pains were too much. Too hard. Back-to-back. The cramping made it hard to breathe. "I can't do this! I can't!" She cried. "Lily, help me! I don't feel so well."

Suddenly, Kelly fell dizzy again. Everything was spinning around and around. She dropped to her knees on the cold mossy ground and knew she was about to pass out.

Sweat dripped from her forehead, and all she could see through her blurry eyes was Lily standing there in front of her, shaking her. "Kelly! KELLY!"

Nothing but darkness answered her back.

Good Girl

Boone headed up the ridge just before dark. He was only given two hours, but there was no way he would make that deadline. It was impossible. Even if he found the girls, he'd never get them back down on time.

He could hear Aunt Sally in his head, say, "Just forget about me. Rescue the girls and leave me there." But he couldn't. How could he leave his aunt with those monsters? He knew what Jimmy would do to her, and he wouldn't let his mind go there.

He had to get to the top of the ridge and back in two hours. There was no other option. He'd just have to pick up the pace. He knew that's where Kelly would go because that's what he taught her to do. Go to the highest point and start a signal fire. It's easier for someone to see. A better chance to be rescued.

Though she knew to head to the highest point, he had no idea how she would be able to do it. She was big and pregnant, and Lily wasn't experienced. They had the baby with them as well, and that meant they would have spent all day trying to get up there.

Boone's heart was sick with worry. Anything could have happened.

He'd been tracking a pack of Alexander Archipelago wolves for a while now, hoping the girls hadn't come across them yet. The coastal wolves were a lot darker than the normal grey wolf and difficult to see in the dark. Hopefully, they made it to the top before them. They should be safe around a fire, at least for now. Boone realized it was getting dark fast, and he had to hurry.

Lord, help my wife. Help me get the girls back within two

hours, or they'll hurt Aunt Sally.

As Boone pushed himself through spruce trees and underbrush, he was losing light. He'd have to improvise. Instead of tracking their steps, he decided to double the pace and head directly to the top. If they made it up there, he'd soon see a fire flicker at the top.

He wondered what would happen when he got the girls back. What would Jimmy do then? First, he couldn't let them take Lily and the Baby. There would be no negotiations. They were not about to let Kelly go, no matter what they said. Guys like Jimmy didn't just let people go. No, he had to come up with a plan fast.

Everyone's life was on the line, including his. He could see it on Jimmy's face. He meant to end him too, just as soon as he brought the girls back to him. It was such a difficult circumstance. If he didn't return with them, Jimmy would surely kill Aunt Sally. If he did return, they would take Lily and the baby, and Kelly would be at risk.

Oh, Lord! It kept circling in his brain. What was the best option? There was none. Think! What he really needed was the National Guard and the Coast Guard. He couldn't rely on the Angoon police department anymore. Though he realized it was probably just Danny and John that were in on this, he didn't really know. There could be more.

Hopefully, Kelly had the fire roaring enough for someone to spot them. If that happened on time, he could rescue Aunt Sally without jeopardizing his wife and Lily and the baby. Surely whoever sees the fire will be able to deal with Jimmy and his thugs as well.

As Boone moved through the bushes, he stopped for a moment. Was that an animal? He heard the grunting sound ahead of him. He slowed his pace to a crawl and ducked down. It was a small brown bear. The place was crawling with wildlife.

It was important to stay downwind from the bear so it couldn't smell him, but on a ridge, it was virtually impossible. He had no way of predicting the wind direction up there. It was very unpredictable. The only thing he could do was keep his eye on it and the wolves. Either way, he had to keep going or he'd run out of time.

Then, to the left of him, he decided to take a trail he found. It looked like the girls had been through there. He saw a diaper and a baby blanket. It was a good thing that he found evidence of them, but worrisome that dangerous animals were on their trail as well.

In a hurry, Boone darted in the opposite direction of the bear and headed up the back side of the ridge. The sun had now set, and he needed to get a move on. Hopefully, soon, he'd see a fire at the top.

This whole traumatic experience brought back bad memories of when he and Kelly got lost in the wilderness after the plane crash. They almost died out there. Between the bears and the Kushtaka, he thought that was the end of them.

Yet, God in His goodness got them through.

Since then, he and Kelly had been through a lot. He knew God hadn't brought them this far to leave them. If one thing was clear, Boone knew the grace of God. He didn't just make your problem disappear. Instead, He helped you through it. Just like God got him through prison, and the plane crash, and the Kushtaka, and all their miscarriages, he knew God would get them through this.

Still, Boone wondered why they always seemed to attract trouble. *What are you doing, Lord?* It all seemed too much. If God considered trials and tribulations a prerequisite for building character, he wondered how much character one person really needed. *Isn't this enough, Lord? Why so many trials?* Surely, they were long overdue for some real blessings.

Boone considered his twins a blessing. He hoped to protect them. They were due very soon, and that meant Kelly could easily go into labour. He hoped that was not the case, because he was not prepared for that. How on earth could he keep them all safe up here?

God, please protect my family!

Then, suddenly, as Boone pushed through to a clearing, he saw a flicker of light at the top of the ridge. It was a large bonfire, just like he hoped to find. His wife must have been paying attention to survival training after all.

Good girl!

Superhero

What was she supposed to do?

It was dark. The fire roared, and baby Charlie was crying in the carrier, strapped to her chest. Kelly had stopped moving and lay on her back in front of her.

Was she dead?

Lily cried and knelt beside Kelly while jiggling the baby to calm his screaming. She touched her lifeless body. It was still warm. She could see she was still breathing. Her chest rose and fell. That wasn't the sign of someone dead.

Between Kelly's legs, she could see blood. It was gross. She didn't want to lift her nightgown to see what was underneath. It reminded her of when Charlie came out and fell into the toilet. Lily didn't want to remember that, but she had no choice. It was right there in front of her, forcing her to feel the same traumatic pain all over again.

She screamed out into the night, in sync with Charlie's frantic dither. There was nowhere to turn. Nobody to help her. She was all alone. Just like always. Just like she tried to tell Kelly, Aunt Sally, and even Boone when he tried to push. *There was no God!* If there was, he wouldn't let stuff like this happen.

"I hate you, God! I HATE YOU! You never help! You didn't help me! You can't help her! You just hurt people! You abandoned me just like everyone else in my life!"

Lily got up and paced around the fire. She could see the town from down below. Why hadn't they seen the signal fire? They were right there. She started humming through sobs, hoping it would calm the baby. She couldn't stand his screaming anymore. She didn't know what else to do. Kelly would know.

She usually took him and calmed him down.

"Shut up, Charlie! Shut up!"

Lily continued to pace around the fire, jiggling the baby, hoping he'd calm down. She left Kelly lying there. She wasn't going anywhere, anyway. At this point, all Lily could think of was that maybe Kelly had passed out from the pain. She remembered her own pain. It was the worst she'd ever felt before. Even she passed out.

Finally, Charlie started to settle down. She could hear him hiccupping. At least she didn't have to worry so much about him. Hopefully, he would fall back asleep. She figured he was probably hungry, but they didn't have any more formula.

Kelly was behind her, warm beside the campfire, when suddenly she heard a noise. It sounded like a growl. Lily turned on her heels and looked over at the woman still lying there motionless, but something was beside her now.

In the shadows, Lily noticed a creature with glowing eyes. It looked like a black wolf. It was circling her, afraid of the fire. "GET AWAY FROM HER!"

Lily rushed over to Kelly's side and grabbed a stick from the fire. She waved it at the wolf, only to reveal more eyes coming forward. There was a pack of them. "LEAVE US ALONE!"

The wolves pressed forward and then retreated as she waved the flaming branch at them. She poked and shouted for them to get back as they pushed forward and backward, taunting her.

They were afraid of the fire, but the big black one focused on Kelly, anyway. Lily grabbed another stick. "Don't you touch her, you stupid thing. GET BACK!"

It looked like the devil himself to Lily. It was a big, black, evil-looking thing with big white fangs. She stood her ground and kept poking at it. Her back was to the flames, just the way Kelly told her to stand if something came at them.

"YOU CAN'T TOUCH US!"

Lily knew what Kelly would say if she were awake. She would tell her to pray. She would spout out her Bible gibberish and get on her knees. Yet, right now, she wondered if trying it her way would do any good.

Probably not. But maybe it was worth a shot.

Even though she and God were on the outs, Lily decided to try. "Okay, God!" she prayed. "If there is a God, PLEASE HELP US!"

The pack of wolves retreated then, surprising Lily. Only the big one inched forward still. She poked both torches at him, but he wouldn't leave Kelly alone. He kept trying to grab her leg. "NO! STOP IT!" Lily directed the flames at him.

"JESUS! PLEASE HELP!"

Lily screamed and waved the torches, but the entire pack swarmed them, circling like a bunch of demons. This was it. She knew it. They were overpowering her again. She couldn't protect Kelly anymore. The big black wolf grabbed Kelly's leg and dragged her away from the fire a little bit at a time.

"NOOO! STOP IT!"

Lily moved over to Kelly and tried to fight the wolves off again. She prayed, "GOD, PLEASE! JESUS, PLEASE HELP!"

The wolf pack retreated once more, and this time, Lily realized they didn't like it when she said the word, *Jesus.* So, she said it again and again. "JESUS, JESUS, JESUS!"

Even the pack leader retreated this time. Lily tried to remember the Bible verse Kelly wanted to pray with her. It was a popular one. She tried to remember the words. "Yea, though I walk through the valley of the shadow of death, I will fear no evil. NO EVIL, MEANS NO EVIL! SO, GET LOST YOU STUPID WOLVES!"

For a moment, Lily stood there panting. Were they gone? Did God do it? She didn't know, but it seemed like it. She looked around, and she couldn't see them anymore. Like a warrior, she stood there with a torch in each hand and a baby attached to her chest. She straddled Kelly's unconscious body and cried up to the heavens. "JESUS! YOU SAVED US!"

It wasn't what Lily expected. It was shocking how the name of Jesus scared them away. Nobody would believe her. How could this be possible? God had never helped her out of anything before. She thought he didn't care. She thought it was just a story.

Why hadn't she cried out to Him before?

Lily howled into the moonlit night, "THANK YOU, JESUS!"

Then, suddenly, from below her feet, Kelly made a noise. She moaned and moved her body slowly. She was alive. God saved Kelly, too.

In the dark of night, flames roaring, Lily realized that God wasn't just a fairytale like she thought. He was real. She just never tried talking to Him before. It was a miracle!

"What's happening?" Kelly spoke in a raspy voice.

"You passed out."

"I did?"

"Lucky thing, too! You missed the wolves."

"What?"

Kelly sat up and moaned with another contraction. Her moaning turned into wailing this time, and Lily knew she was in trouble. This time, she wasn't going to cower. She felt invincible, like a superhero with special God powers or something. She'd never felt like this before. It was amazing!

"God will help you!"

Kelly cocked her head as she panted out of breath. "I hope so, because something is seriously wrong with me!"

"I can tell."

Kelly sobbed. She shook her head and held her belly. "Maybe the babies are stuck?" She panted and tried to breathe through the tears.

Lily bit her lip and wondered if she should put her new superpowers to work. If she could push past the fear, maybe she could actually be useful. "How can I help?"

"PRAY!"

I Can't

Boone could hear the commotion. It sounded like someone was dying. He rushed to get up there as fast as he could. The fire appeared to be roaring, and that was a good thing. But what was happening?

The worst nightmares danced through his head. It could be anything.

The wolves may have found them. *Oh, Lord! No!* He wouldn't let his mind go there. Instead, he focused on moving through the underbrush and tangled trees in front of him as quickly as possible. He was almost there.

As soon as he pushed passed them through the clearing, something met him at the top. It was the wolf pack. They were retreating from something and running straight into him. There were about six of them, surrounding him with glowing eyes.

All he had was a knife.

"GET!" he told them.

Boone pulled the hidden knife from his leg holster and realized it wasn't a match for the six of them. He kicked at them and held his knife securely.

One at a time, they came at him, as he sliced at them in defence. There was an alpha who wasn't giving in. This one was mean. He bared his teeth and growled as the others seemed to back off. It was a standoff.

"God, please help me!"

Boone didn't even have time to think. He knew a knife wouldn't ward them off. They didn't even know what a knife was. "Leave me alone!" he shouted. Instead, the alpha male just moved closer, growling with bared teeth.

Suddenly, the beast leaped at him and took him down. He landed hard on his shoulder as the wolf bit into his left arm. With his right arm, he stabbed the thing in the neck, over and over, until it fell limp.

Boone sat on the ground and panted. Was it really over? Had he killed the alpha? Would the others defend him now? He didn't know. He just wiped his brow and pulled the bloodied knife from the carcass.

It was dark, but the moonlight allowed him to see the carnage he had left behind. He had killed three of them. He was lucky. Though Boone realized this had nothing to do with luck. It was all God. He knew that by now.

Then, in the distance, by the flicker of the fire he viewed, he heard another sound. It was moaning. It sounded like someone in pain. Was it Kelly? Were they hurt? He got up, dusted himself off, and stuffed the knife back in his leg holster.

"KELLY!" he shouted.

"Boone!" A voice answered back.

It wasn't Kelly, it was Lilly. And he could hear Charlie's cries echo into the night. He ran as fast as he could over to them, hoping to find his wife alive. "KELLY!"

All Boone could hear was moaning and crying. Did the wolf attack her? He pushed harder to get to them on the other side of the clearing. "What happened?"

As soon as Boone arrived, he knew.

"She's having the babies."

"Kelly! Talk to me!"

Kelly sat on the ground, moaning and hyperventilating. "I'm sorry! The babies. They're coming!"

"You're okay!"

Boone knelt at her side and assessed her. He put his First Aid/CPR certification to use and made sure she was okay. Other than the bite on her right calf, she seemed okay. She was in active labour, and it looked like she was dragged by a wolf as well. That didn't sit well with him.

Her nightgown was bloody and dirty, and he realized she

must be freezing. "Here! Put this on. He stripped his heavy-duty hunting jacket off his body and wrapped it around his wife.

"Lily? Are you okay?"

"I'm okay, but Charlie's crying again. He's so hungry."

"As long as he's not injured, he's fine. One thing at a time, okay? Tell me how long she's been like this. Kells? When did your contractions start?"

Kelly wasn't responding. She just shook her head and cried in delirium.

"She's been like this all day. She even passed out for about ten minutes."

Boone sighed to himself, *What now, Lord?*

It was only a matter of time before the babies would come. They weren't prepared for this. Not here. Not in the middle of the wilderness. "Lily, find anything you can burn and throw it on the fire. We're going to make it big and loud. Do you hear me?"

"I gathered some branches earlier. And we found some logs over there. We've been feeding the fire pretty good. Do you think someone will see it?"

"They have to!"

Boone knew it was a long shot. He dragged the logs the girls had found and threw them on the fire. He even threw the stumps they were sitting on into the fire. "Everything! Let's go!"

The two of them worked at the fire steadily as Kelly sat on the ground, moaning. Charlie wailed loudly, which didn't help matters much.

Then, for a moment, Lily stopped and looked at him. "Boone! It will be okay. I prayed!"

Boone nodded and kept going. He was glad to hear the girl finally had a conversation with the Lord. Her childlike faith was endearing, but he also knew everything fell on his shoulders now. *God, I want to believe, but how are you going to get us out of here?*

He knew he only had a half-hour to get them back down the ridge to save his aunt, yet it wasn't happening now. He had to choose. It was either his wife and unborn children or his aunt. He could carry Lily and the baby down the ridge in double-time and get there to complete the deal, or stay up there and help his wife.

There was no question what he had to do, and it broke his heart.

Take care of my Aunt Sally, Jesus. I didn't want to give up on her.

"So, Kells..." he cleared his throat and focused on his wife. "I'm going to need you to lie down. I'm sorry, honey. I have to check if the baby is ready to come out. Lily, stand on guard. If anything moves, you need to tell me."

"Got it!"

Boone shoved Kelly's arms into his jacket to keep her warm and made her lie down. He lifted her nightgown to see if the head was visible. He'd never done this before, except for reading it in books. Emergency childbirth wasn't covered in First Aid class, but he would have to wing it, one step at a time.

From what he could see from the campfire light, the head wasn't even visible yet. It looked like she had a long way to go. The amount of blood alarmed him, though, and that made him worry. *Someone find us!*

Boone covered her with her nightgown again and helped her sit up. "Do you feel like the baby is coming out? I can't see the head, so I don't think you should push yet. But I don't know for sure. I just see a lot of blood."

"SOMETHING'S WRONG!"

"Kells, I want you to look at me. BREATHE! ONE! TWO! THREE! In and out. You can do this. If you feel like pushing, then maybe you should push!"

"I CAN'T DO THIS!"

"*Yea, though I walk through the valley of the shadow of death,*" Lily prayed as she paced back and forth, "*I will fear no evil. Thy rod and thy staff they comfort me.*"

"Thank you, Lily!"

Boone tried to comfort his wife, but he didn't know what

else to do. She was exhausted. She looked like she was about to pass out again. "And she's been like this all day, you say?"

"Well, not this bad. This is the worst. She gets like this, and then she starts shaking. That's what happened last time. Then she passes out. Is she going to pass out again?"

"I hope not. Just go stand guard, please."

The fire roared, and Charlie cried, and Boone was at his wits' end. He knew that God was in control, but he also knew bad things still happened. Maybe that meant he just didn't have enough faith. He struggled with this so much.

Help my unbelief.

Boone coached Kelly through the next few contractions, but nothing had changed. She seemed to have a lot of pain without any progress. Maybe Kelly was right and something was wrong. He wasn't a doctor and didn't know the right way to do this. He didn't want to tell her the wrong thing, but maybe she just needed to start pushing. He'd coach her to do that with the next contraction.

Boone grabbed the baby blankets from the diaper bag just in case. If she gave birth now, he'd have to keep them warm somehow.

Oh God! Please help! This could end badly.

"Okay, Kelly! On your next contraction, I want you to push!"

"I CAN'T!"

"You can!"

Then, from the corner of his eye, he saw Lily run to his side.

"Um! Boone!"

"What is it?"

"You'd better come look."

Boone sighed and stood up. He looked to where Lily was pointing just inside the tree line. It was the small bear he saw earlier.

JUST GREAT!

Sacrifice

Boone was hoping the bear would leave them alone. He figured they had no choice but to ignore it. As long as they kept their distance, he figured they had nothing to worry about.

It looked like a small female, and that meant she was just foraging for torpor. She was likely pregnant and had a den nearby, ready for a good sleep. If they left her alone, she would probably go away. By now, she would have been feasting long enough to build up her fat storage.

If he was right, they'd be lucky.

"Don't look at her. Just let her be," Boone told Lily. "I know it's alarming, but we have to ignore her. Try not to worry."

"Worry?" Lily snapped, "How am I not supposed to worry? IT'S A BEAR!"

"The worst thing you could do is run, so DON'T! Just stay close to me, and stay by the fire. It will go away."

"You better be right!"

Boone was more concerned with Kelly than he was with Lily. She would stay by him, but Kelly was bleeding. It wasn't a lot, but it was enough to get the bear to notice. Their sense of smell was exceptional, and that concerned him. There was nothing he could do about it, though.

All he could do was give it to the Lord.

Kelly continued to moan and cry in pain. It now seemed to be one long continuous contraction. He didn't know what to do. Not only was the blood attracting the bear, but it was also causing it to move closer. Either it was being curious, or aggravated by the constant howling from his wife. Even the baby crying was triggering the bear.

"It's coming closer."

"I know. I know."

Boone got up and assessed the situation. He knew better than to challenge the animal, but he got his knife out just in case. Not that it would protect them from it at all, but it would give them a fighting chance at least. Where was bear spray when you needed it?

It was then that he noticed his arm was dripping blood as well. The wolf tore it up pretty good. The last time something attacked his arm, it didn't end well. His veins were already shot in that arm. Hopefully, it would hold out, but it gave the bear something more to smell, and that was not good. The whole group smelled good to the bear.

"Don't leave me, Boone!" Lily called after him.

"I need to scare it away."

"Don't!"

"Lily, just stay put. I'll be right back."

"Maybe we should pray. Please Boone! Don't leave me!"

The girl was right. "Okay, grab my hand." He held Kelly's hand, too. She looked up and moaned, looking like a zombie. The poor woman had been through too much. This whole thing was too much. He would lead them in a prayer, and then go deal with the bear. If it was the last thing he did, he'd fight the bear to protect them.

Even if he had to sacrifice himself to do it.

Boone recited a Bible verse from memory. *"Be strong and courageous. Do not be afraid or terrified because of the bear."* He added the bear part, more for himself because of what he was about to do. *"For the Lord your God goes with you; he will never leave you nor forsake you."*

The bear crept closer. It was now or never.

"Look!" Lily cried, "The bear is stomping and huffing. What do we do?"

Boone knew what that meant, and he knew what he had to do. He quickly kissed his wife on the cheek, put his hand on her stomach and said a silent goodbye. He put his hand on Lily's shoulder and said, "Take care of them!"

"Wait, wait!" the girl cried. "Stay here!"

"I can't. If I do, the bear will kill us all."

"But what about you?"

Boone looked her in the eye and said nothing. Hopefully, she understood that he didn't have a choice. He had to lead the bear away. It was their only hope.

"Hey bear!" Boone suddenly shouted, waving his arms. "Come here!" He made a huffing sound and taunted the bear away from the women. Then he started running.

The bear was following him all the way to the edge of the clearing. It was a stupid move on Boone's part when he realized there was a drop-off ledge he hadn't anticipated. He trapped himself between that and the bear. It was either jump off the cliff or get attacked.

Boone decided on the latter. There was no way he'd survive a thirty-foot drop. At least with the bear, he had half a chance with his knife.

The bear swatted him across the back, sending him flying. He dropped his knife but picked it up before the bear came at him again. This time, Boone lunged at the animal, slicing it across the nose. He was aiming for her eye.

That made her even madder. She galloped over to him and swatted him with her paw. Immediately, Boone rolled over on his stomach, but then the Bear stepped on his back. He turned to his side when she stepped off, and he quickly stabbed her in the neck. A gush of warm blood ran down his arm.

The bear was stunned.

That gave him a minute to get up and run as fast as he could. There was no playing dead with this one. She was smart. He was the underdog. His only hope was to get away.

Boone took a beeline to the trees across the clearing, far away from the girls and the fire. If he could get to the trees, maybe he could climb. Even though his body ached from the pummelling, he still had strength. He could climb if he could

KATHLEEN MORRIS

only get there.

But the bear was gaining on him.

It was just a foot away when Boone heard a shot ring out. Someone hit the bear. It tumbled and rolled just inches away from him. They almost tangled together.

Then, above, Boone saw a chopper hover. It beamed its spotlight on the bear, illuminating the carnage below. The bear was dead. He was alive.

Thank you, God!

Boone squinted into the spotlight, cupping his bloody, shaking hand over his brow as he looked above. Two choppers hovered over him. *Praise the Lord!* One was an air ambulance, and the other was the Coast Guard.

Finally!

He dropped to his knees and waved them down. The Coast Guard chopper set down first. Once the blades slowed and the chopper door opened, Boone saw the officers jump out and run toward him. Then, behind them, he saw a familiar face jump out as well. He was never more glad to see her friendly face.

Aunt Sally!

Battle Wounds

The medical crew went to Kelly immediately. They assessed her and loaded her into the chopper. Their level of professionalism was a comfort to Boone, especially knowing they had all the equipment on board to help her.

They bandaged his arm in the field and assessed his broken ribs and banged-up body, telling him he was lucky to be alive. He was to climb on board the Coast Guard helicopter with Lily and the baby, and his Aunt Sally.

But first, he wanted to know what was happening with his wife.

"We're setting down in Angoon first," the paramedic told him. "You're doctor has his staff on stand-by at the clinic. We'll assess the rest of it from there."

"Is she going to be okay? What about the twins?"

"We'll do everything we can. She has some complications. I'm sorry. We'll know more when we get her to the clinic. You can follow." The paramedic pointed to the other chopper and waved that they were about to take off. Boone backed away from the whirring propellers as he watched them lift his entire life into the air.

God, don't let me lose her.

He ran over to the other chopper and eased his beaten body on board. His Aunt Sally pulled him to sit down, and she leaned over to hold him.

"It will be okay!"

Boone fought back tears as the chopper roared to life. As they rose, he could see the bear carcass lying there where they shot it, thankful for their intervention. If not for them, he'd be dead right now. The carnage below slowly faded as his thoughts focused on his wife.

He could lose everything...again.

"Let's pray!" Aunt Sally said, grabbing Boone's good hand and Lily's hand beside her. "It's in times like these that Jesus carries us. Just as sure as this chopper carries us now, Jesus carries us through every storm. There is nothing He can't do. Do you hear me? *Nothing!*"

His aunt prayed for Kelly's safety. She prayed for his unborn children. She prayed for Lily. She prayed for Charlie in the air ambulance under medical watch. Finally, she recited her favourite Bible verse, the one he had prayed with Lily earlier. Go figure, his aunt is the one who taught him how to quote verses specific to the need. *Thank you, Aunt Sally!*

"Do not be afraid or terrified because of Kelly's condition," Aunt Sally prayed. *"For the Lord your God goes with you; he will never leave you nor forsake you."*

Lily started to cry then. Aunt Sally looked up and gave her a sideways hug. "You know this is true now, don't you?"

Lily nodded through sobs.

"Then we're all good, aren't we?"

Boone fought off tears while the chopper hovered over the Angoon Heliport at the clinic, just about to land. It's where they just took Kelly. He was eager to get inside.

"Now, Boone," Aunt Sally directed him like a mother, "I want you to let them do their work. Whatever happens here, I will be right by your side. You are never alone."

Boone burst into tears now, unable to hold it back any longer. He was thankful for his aunt, who took the place of his mother so long ago. She was also good at comforting. The two sisters were like twins themselves.

Twins! Don't let me lose them either, Lord!

As soon as they landed, Boone rushed ahead of everyone and down a corridor to the front desk. "Kelly! WHERE IS SHE?"

The receptionist pointed down another hall.

Boone shot off as fast as his beaten body would take him.

He was greeted at the end of the hall by the paramedics who brought her in. "Hey, hey! Slow down! She's in good hands."

"WHAT'S HAPPENING?"

"Well, you're lucky your doctor flew his staff up here yesterday. They were all prepared for an emergency C-section when we got here. That's gotta be a first for this little clinic."

"CAN I GO IN?"

"No, nobody's allowed through these doors."

Boone paced back and forth, raking his hand through his red hair. He bit his lip and shook his head, remembering what his aunt told him. 'Let them do their work.'

It was hard, but he had to back off. There was nothing he could do but wait. God had a funny way of teaching patience. He didn't remove the stress most of the time, just helped you through it. This is what his aunt meant by Jesus carrying you. Oh, so true.

"Let Him have it," she would say.

Aunt Sally and Lily finally arrived then. "Come! Sit down, my boy!" She led him to the nearest chairs. "What good will you be if you pass out? Besides, we're all in line to see the doctor. Especially you. Look at you!"

Boone didn't care about his own pain, even though he could barely breathe through his broken ribs. Being stomped on by a 400-pound grizzly wasn't exactly a cakewalk.

"I'm fine," he winced.

"Sure you are," Aunt Sally laughed. "My boy, you are the worst liar I've ever seen."

Boone winced again as he cracked a smile. "Don't make me laugh, aunty!"

"Why not? It sure beats crying."

"You should see him at home," Lily smiled. "He doesn't know how to be a wimp."

"Hey, you!" Boone winked at the girl. He was glad she lightened the mood. It took his mind off the current stress. For the first time, he had a moment to breathe. He looked at his aunt and noticed the bruises on her face.

She must have gone through hell with Jimmy and his gang. Speaking of that. He needed some answers. "I'm sorry they did this to you, Aunty. You didn't deserve this."

"None of us did, my boy." Aunt Sally nodded.

Boone rested a hand on his aunt and then Lily, giving a nod that he understood. None of this should have happened to any of them. He still beat himself up that he couldn't stop it from happening, especially to the people he loved.

"So, what happened to you, Aunty? How did you get away?"

"Boone, you wouldn't believe it. When I say God has things under control, I mean it. About half an hour after you left, we were surrounded. There was a standoff. I have never been more proud of our little Angoon police department than I was at that moment. Boone, they came through! John...he would have been so proud of them."

John.

A moment of silence followed her statement. Boone wished he could have gotten through to the guy. It didn't have to end with him being killed. A pension wasn't worth his life. It was just money. Easy for him to say, but John couldn't get over it. He was in too deep, and he didn't know how to get out. Not to mention, he was probably ashamed.

It was sad.

Boone took a breath and composed himself. Taking in what she just said. "So, they got 'em? Jimmy? All of them?"

"Danny's dead."

Boone shook his head. The guy's involvement still shocked him.

"And Jimmy?"

"They arrested him and the others. I'm sure Jimmy's going to jail for a very long time...again. This time, he isn't getting out."

Boone sat there and took it all in. His buddy crossed the line way too many times. It finally caught up with him. He was glad they got him. Yet, somewhere in the back of his mind, he felt a twinge of sympathy.

It was bittersweet.

After all, the guy used to be his friend. In another lifetime, he remembered the fun hunting trips they had. It was a real shame how he turned out. Had it not been for the Lord, Boone would have turned out just the same.

Maybe.

Jimmy was crazy. He was not. A sociopath never changes. He keeps getting worse. You can't teach someone to have empathy or remorse. Either you have it or you don't. Boone was glad they got him off the streets.

After about an hour of waiting, they were each brought into an exam room. Aunt Sally was fine. Her bruises would heal. She was referred to a trauma counsellor. It was the same with Lily. Charlie was still being monitored to make sure he was okay. They fed him and told Aunt Sally if she was up to it, she could take both Lily and Charlie home as soon as they got word about Kelly.

They were still waiting.

As for Boone, they took him in for an X-ray. He had three broken ribs. He was told it would be a long recovery. Broken rib pain is excruciating. One of the worst kinds of pain. He knew that from experience. Yet, he didn't care. His pain was nothing compared to what his wife went through.

"Is she still in surgery?"

"I'm sorry, Mr. McKenzie, I don't know. We haven't heard a thing."

Boone bit his lip. No news was usually good news, but under the circumstances, it didn't sound good. Surely, it wouldn't be much longer.

"Let me know as soon as you know anything!"

"We will."

Boone went back to the waiting room and sat with his aunt and Lily. He shrugged when they asked him if he had heard anything. They weren't surprised to hear he had three broken ribs.

"You can add that to your battle wounds, my boy."

"Funny!"

"Kelly won't be surprised. She knows you."

Silence set in with the mention of his wife's name. They were all worried. They were all just passing the time. *Lord, I need to know,*" he prayed silently. "Is she okay?"

Nothing answered him back. He sighed and shut his eyes. He was more tired than he's ever been in his life, yet sleep seemed forbidden at a time like this.

Then, after another two hours had dragged on, a nurse finally came running down the hallway. "Sir? Are you Boone McKenzie?"

"Yah!" He stood up, alarmed.

"Can you come with me?"

"Why? What's happening?"

The others stood up too, listening to the conversation. Boone turned to his Aunt Sally with wide eyes as he held her hand. She reassured him that it would be okay. But would it be? Her faith was obviously a lot stronger than his.

"Is she okay?"

"I-I'm sorry, I'm just the messenger. You need to hurry."

HURRY?

Jesus, don't let this be bad news.

Double Portion

They brought Boone into a private room where Kelly was lying on the table. She seemed lifeless. She was hooked up to an IV and all kinds of beeping machines. He didn't know what was happening.

"Kelly?" He tried to speak to her, but she wasn't responding.

A nurse came in and hung another IV bag. She didn't speak to him, and that alarmed him. Why weren't they talking to him?

"Is she okay?"

The nurse bit her lip and just said, "The doctor will be with you shortly."

Boone examined her bruised face and brushed the back of his hand against her soft, warm skin. She looked so peaceful lying there. He moved his hand over her abdomen, and the babies were gone.

What had happened to them? Where was the doctor? They told him to hurry. Why? What was the rush when nobody was even in there to talk to him?

Then, Dr Thomas himself entered the room. He must have flown in with his staff. The man was a saint. "I'm so sorry, Boone. You must be sick with worry. I needed to use the washroom before I spoke with you. Please forgive me for the lack of communication. This was a difficult surgery, and we wanted to make sure we got it all right before calling you in."

"Got it all right? What do you mean? Just tell me...is she going to be okay?"

"Yes, but I need to explain what happened," Dr. Thomas

said. "She had a postpartum hemorrhage after the C-section. She lost a great deal of blood. Boone, we almost lost her twice."

"But she's going to make it...right?"

"Yes, she's stable now. She's lucky to be alive, but we had to take the uterus. I'm sorry. There was nothing we could do."

Boone looked at the man who saved his wife's life and tried to figure out what he was really trying to say. Was he telling him the twins didn't make it? Was this it? Were they never going to have a family? She could live without a uterus, but not without the twins. That would destroy her. *That would destroy him.*

"What about our twins?"

The doctor patted him on the back. "Well...you got one heck of a fighter."

"Just ONE?"

Dr. Thomas smiled and re-adjusted his glasses. Boone forgot how the guy liked to draw out a story. Even in a situation like this, he was still a storyteller.

"TWO, I mean two! They are both holding their own. We had to fly them out right away. I'm sorry. We couldn't inform you because Kelly was crashing for the second time. We had to focus on her, and we didn't want to tell you anything until she pulled through. I'm sorry."

"No, you did the right thing. Are they going to Anchorage?"

"Yes, neonatal is on standby for them as we speak."

"So...they're healthy then?"

"Boone, I'm not going to lie. It was touch-and-go with both of them, too. The first one, she's a fighter. She was trying to come out breach, you know. Your wife must have gone through a lot of pain with no progress and a lot of back labour. The second twin was in a posterior position. Both were unfavourable. We had to get them out quickly. They were in fetal distress, and their heart rates dropped.

Boone scratched his head. Wasn't that bad? Were they going to be okay or not? The doctor's long, drawn-out story was starting to annoy him. All he wanted was a simple answer.

"Doctor, please. I just need to know. Are they okay?"

"Oh, me and my big mouth. I'm sorry."

"Well?"

"Yes, yes. They both had an APGAR score of 7 when all was said and done, so they're doing fine. No oxygen deprivation. Someone was watching over these two little sweethearts. But they are premature, though, so they need neonatal support for a few weeks. Other than their heart rates dropping and their tricky entry into this world, they seem to be doing remarkably well."

Praise the Lord!

"Thank you, doctor, for saving my family," Boone teared up. "I don't know what we would have done without you and your staff. We owe you everything!"

"Boone, it was my pleasure. Really, it was. I take good care of my two favourite patients. We have a lot of history together. I consider you guys my friends, not just my patients. That's why I flew in to join my staff. How could I *not* be here?"

Boone hugged Dr. Thomas and then shook his hand. He was thankful the Lord brought such a kind-hearted man into their lives.

"Now what? Where do we go from here?"

"Well...now. That was why we called you in here so fast.

Then, a nurse came in, all out of breath. "Doctor, they're here," she interrupted their conversation. He looked at his watch and filled him in on the details.

"The Juneau air ambulance is on a tight schedule. Their ETA was five minutes, and they said we'd better be ready. And here I am blabbering again. They won't forgive me, you know," he winked. "They always tell me I'm too long-winded."

"I wonder why that is?" Boone teased him. "So, Kelly is okay to fly like this?"

"She's stable. I've sedated her for the trip. It should take approximately two hours. I'm going with you, you know. I cleared my schedule for you guys."

"Thank you!"

The doctor nodded. "We'll go by helicopter to Juneau. You know, the usual thirty minutes. Then, we'll take a charter to Anchorage. That takes about an hour and a half."

"And the twins?"

"Like I said, we rushed them out of here with the first chopper. I had a medical plane waiting in Juneau on standby for them. The infants should be in the neonatal unit soon. We'll get word when we're in flight. Relax, Boone. I've done this before."

Boone tried to breathe. Like he said, the man was a saint. A very long-winded one, but he knew his stuff. It was a pleasure to have a doctor treat you so well. These days, other doctors are so rushed, they barely know your name.

"Are you ready?" the doctor asked. "Let's move, people." He directed his staff to push the bed into the hallway and down the corridor.

"Oh, wait!" Boone stopped them. "My aunt." He saw her and Lily standing in the hallway watching the whole thing. "Can I have a minute?"

An annoyed paramedic stopped in front of him and looked at his watch. "You got two minutes, buddy. Then, we leave without you."

"NO!" Dr. Thomas scolded him. "Have some respect. You have no idea what these people just went through. You will give him as long as he needs."

The paramedic shook his head and swore under his breath.

"Two minutes! I promise!" Boone repeated.

He hurried up to his Aunt Sally and Lily and hugged them both. He couldn't hold back the tears. "We got two healthy baby girls. I'll fill you in once we're in flight. Kelly's okay. She's okay. She's sedated, and we gotta go. The babies are already there."

"Where are you going?" Lily asked.

"Anchorage."

"That place has a lot of bad memories."

"Well, we're gonna change that!" The three of them

hugged in a circle. Aunt Sally led with God's word. He would remember it for the rest of his life.

"And after you have suffered a little while, the God of all grace, who has called you to his eternal glory in Christ, will himself restore, confirm, strengthen, and establish you."

"Amen!"

"What does that mean?" Lily asked.

"It means the Lord will restore everything the devil took from you, my dear!" Aunt Sally smiled. "Just you wait and see."

Boone nodded. He couldn't believe the miracles that took place this day. He couldn't believe the miracles that were waiting for him.

"And Jesus!" His aunt added, "Thank you for taking good care of us! And help Boone remember how you restored Job."

"Thank you!" Boone smiled.

"And one more thing..." Aunt Sally wasn't done yet. He grinned and let her finish. He knew better than to cut this woman short. She was adamant about scripture. She taught him well, and now it would be his turn to teach his own kids.

"You'd better hurry up, Aunty. We got one angry paramedic staring us down."

"Oh, let him. We'll pray for him too."

Boone prayed for the man and all his friends. Everyone who helped in this horrible crisis. He was thankful Jesus carried them all through the storm.

"And now the scripture I found in Job fits right in...with a little twist that is," she winked. *"And the Lord restored the fortunes of Boone when he prayed for his friends. And the Lord gave Boone twice as much as he had before."*

"Amen!"

"Now, go get your double portion!"

THE END

* * *

Lost in Kootznoowoo – (Book 1 in the Fatherless

Series) Available on Amazon

How to Become a Christian

The Bible says we are saved by grace through faith in Jesus Christ. (Ephesians 2:8-9). We don't have to earn our salvation by working for it. Grace Alone. Faith Alone.
Salvation is simple, like the ABCs.
A –ADMIT you are a sinner. "For all have sinned and fall short of the glory of God. (Romans 3:23).
B – BELIEVE in Jesus. "For God so loved the world that he gave his one and only Son, that whoever believes in him shall not perish but have eternal life." (John 3:16).
C – CONFESS that Jesus is your Lord. "If we confess our sins, he is faithful and just and will forgive us our sins and purify us from all unrighteousness." (1 John 1:9).

Romans 10:13 – "Everyone who calls on the name of the Lord will be saved."

The Salvation Prayer
Dear Jesus, I admit that I am a sinner and in need of a Saviour. I believe with all my heart that you are the Son of God who died and rose again for me. You took my punishment, so I don't have to. You made me clean by your finished work on the cross. Today, I acknowledge that salvation is not of my own doing, but is by grace through faith alone. It is a free gift to me, and I accept that gift. You are my Lord and Saviour forever! Thank you!

Congratulations!
If you prayed this prayer and you believe it with all your heart, you are now a believer! Remember to talk to him every day. That's how you have a relationship with Him. His spirit will

guide you and help you!

Follow Him all the days of your life!

About the Author

Kathleen Morris is a Christian author of Evangelical fiction, both in romantic suspense and thrillers. She loves to write about Biblical truths and show how her characters find Christ through traumatic circumstances. She writes for ministry and loves the art of storytelling. Kathleen makes her home in Saskatchewan, Canada, and loves spending time with her husband, children and grandchildren. It is her hope and dream to be used by God to spread the gospel through her writing.

For Kathleen Morris' books, go to Amazon.com.